I0631284

William Dean Howells

Out of the Question

A Comedy

William Dean Howells

Out of the Question
A Comedy

ISBN/EAN: 9783744661539

Printed in Europe, USA, Canada, Australia, Japan

Cover: Foto ©Andreas Hilbeck / pixelio.de

More available books at **www.hansebooks.com**

Out of the Question.

A COMEDY.

BY

W. D. HOWELLS.

BOSTON:
JAMES R. OSGOOD AND COMPANY.
Late Ticknor & Fields, and Fields, Osgood, & Co.
1877.

Copyright, 1877,

By H. O. Houghton & Co. and W. D. Howells.

RIVERSIDE, CAMBRIDGE:

STEREOTYPED AND PRINTED BY

H. O. HOUGHTON AND COMPANY.

CONTENTS.

I.

IN THE PARLOR OF THE PONKWASSET HOTEL.

OUT OF THE QUESTION.

I.

Miss Maggie Wallace *and* Miss Lilly Roberts.

The Ponkwasset Hotel stands on the slope of a hill and fronts the irregular mass of Ponkwasset Mountain, on which the galleries and northern windows of the parlor look out. The parlor is furnished with two hair-cloth sofas, two hair-cloth easy-chairs, and cane-seated .chairs of divers patterns; against one side of the room stands a piano, near either end of which a door opens into the corridor; in the center of the parlor a marble-topped table supports a state-lamp of kerosene, — a perfume by day, a flame by night, — and near this table sit two young ladies with what they call work in their hands and laps.

Miss Maggie Wallace, with her left wrist curved in the act of rolling up a part of her work, at which she looks down with a very thoughtful air and a careworn little sigh: "I don't think I shall cut it bias, after all, Lilly."

Miss Lilly Roberts, letting her work fall into her lap, in amazement: "Why, Maggie!"

Maggie: "No. Or at least I shan't decide to do so till I've had Leslie's opinion on it. *She* has *perfect* taste, and she could tell at a glance whether it would do."

Lilly: "I wonder she isn't here, now. The stage must be very late."

Maggie: "I suppose the postmaster at South Herodias waited to finish his supper before he 'changed the mail,' as they call it. I *was* so in hopes she would come while they were at *tea!* It will *so* disgust her to see them all strung along the piazza and staring their eyes out at the arrivals, when the stage drives up," — a horrible picture which Miss Wallace dreamily contemplates for a moment in mental vision.

Lilly: "Why don't you go down, too, Maggie? Perhaps she'd find a familiar face a relief."

Maggie, recalled to herself by the wild sugges-
tion : " Thank you, Lilly. I'd rather not be
thought so vulgar as *that*, by Leslie Bellingham,
if it's quite the same to other friends. Imagine
her catching sight of me in that crowd! I should
simply wither away."

Lilly, rebelliously : " Well, I don't see why she
should feel authorized to overawe people in that
manner. What does she do to show her immense
superiority ? "

Maggie : " Everything! In the first place she's
so refined and cultivated, you can't live ; and then
she takes your breath away, she's so perfectly
lovely ; and then she kills you dead with her style,
and all that. She isn't the least stiff. She's the
kindest to other people you ever saw, and the care-
fullest of their feelings ; and she has the grand-
est principles, and she's *divinely* impulsive! But
somehow you feel that if you do anything that's a
little vulgar in her presence, you'd better die at
once. It was always so at school, and it always
will be. Why you would no more dare to do or
say anything just a little common, don't you know,

with Leslie Bellingham " — A young lady, tall, slender, and with an air of delicate distinction, has appeared at the door of the parlor. She is of that type of beauty which approaches the English, without losing the American fineness and grace ; she is fair, and her eyes are rather gray than blue ; her nose is slightly aquiline ; her expression is serious, but becomes amused as she listens to Miss Wallace. She wears one of those blonde traveling-costumes, whose general fashionableness she somehow subdues into character with herself ; over her arm she carries a shawl. She drifts lightly into the room. At the rustling of her dress Miss Wallace looks up, and with a cry of surprise and ecstasy springs from her chair, scattering the contents of her work-box in every direction over the floor, and flings herself into Miss Leslie Bellingham's embrace. Then she starts away from her and gazes rapturously into her face, while they prettily clasp hands and hold each other at arm's length : " Leslie! You heard every word! "

Miss Leslie Bellingham, Maggie, *and* Lilly.

Leslie: "Every syllable, my child. And when you came to my grand principles, I simply said to myself, 'Then listening at keyholes is heroic,' and kept on eavesdropping without a murmur. Had you quite finished?"

Maggie: "O Leslie! You know I *never* can finish when I get on that subject! It inspires me to greater and greater flights every minute. Where is your *mother?* Where *is* Mrs. Murray? Where is the *stage?* Why, excuse me! This is Miss Roberts. Lilly, it's Leslie Bellingham! *Oh*, how glad I am to see you together at last! Did n't the stage" —

Leslie, having graciously bowed to Miss Roberts: "No, Maggie. The stage did n't bring me here. I walked."

Maggie : " Why, Leslie! How perfectly ghastly !"

Leslie : " The stage has done nothing but disgrace itself ever since we left the station. In the first place it pretended to carry ten or twelve people and their baggage, with two horses. Four horses ought n't to drag such a load up these precipices ; and wherever the driver would stop for me, I insisted upon getting out to walk."

Maggie : " How like you, Leslie ! "

Leslie : " Yes ; I wish the resemblance were not so striking. I 'm here in character, Maggie, if you like, but almost nothing else. I 've nothing but a hand-bag to bless me with for the next twenty-four hours. Shall you be very much ashamed of me ?"

Maggie : " Why, you don't mean to say you 've lost your trunks ? Horrors ! "

Leslie : " No. I mean that I was n't going to let the driver add them to the cruel load he had already, and I made him leave them at the station till to-morrow night."

Maggie, embracing her : "Oh, you dear, good, grand, generous Leslie! How — Why, but Leslie! He'll have *just* as many people to-morrow night, and your trunks besides theirs!"

Leslie, with decision: "Very well! Then I shall not be there to see the outrage. I will not have suffering or injustice of any kind inflicted in my presence, if I can help it. That is all." Nevertheless, Miss Bellingham sinks into one of the arm-chairs with an air of some dismay, and vainly taps the toe of her boot with the point of her umbrella in a difficult interval of silence.

Maggie, finally: "But where is your hand-bag?"

Leslie, with mystery, "Oh, *he's* bringing it."

Maggie: "He?"

Leslie, with reviving spirits: "A young man, the good genius of the drive. He's bringing it from the foot of the hill; the stage had its final disaster there; and I left him in charge of mamma and aunt Kate, and came on to explore and sur-prise, and he made me leave the bag with him, too. But that is n't the worst. I shall know what to do with the hand-bag when it gets here, but I shan't know what to do with the young man."

Maggie: "With the young man? Why, Leslie,

a young man is worth a *thousand* hand-bags in a place like this! You don't know what you're talking about, Leslie. A young man "—

Leslie, rising and going toward the window: "My dear, he's out of the question. You may as well make up your mind to that, for you'll see at once that he'll never do. He's going to stop here, and as he's been very kind to us it makes his never doing all the harder to manage. He's a hero, if you like, but if you can imagine it he isn't quite — well, what you've been used to. Don't you see how a person could be everything that was unselfish and obliging, and yet not — not "—

Maggie, eagerly: "Oh yes!"

Leslie : "Well, he's that. It seems to me that he's been doing something for mamma, or aunt Kate, or me, ever since we left the station. To begin with, he gave up his place inside to one of us, and when he went to get on top, he found all the places taken there ; and so he had to sit on the trunks behind — whenever he rode ; for he walked most of the way, and helped me over the bad places in the road when I insisted on getting out.

You know how aunt Kate is, Maggie, and how many wants she has. Well, there was n't one of them that this young man did n't gratify: he handed her bag up to the driver on top because it crowded her, and handed it down because she could n't do without it; he got her out and put her back so that she could face the front, and then restored her to her place because an old gentleman who had been traveling a long way kept falling asleep on her shoulder; he buttoned her curtain down because she was sure it was going to rain, and rolled it up because it made the air too close; he fetched water for her; he looked every now and then to see if her trunks were all right, and made her more and more ungrateful every minute. Whenever the stage broke down — as it did twice before the present smash-up — he befriended everybody, encouraged old ladies, quieted children, and shamed the other men into trying to be of some use; and if it had n't been for him, I don't see how the stage would ever have got out of its troubles; he always knew just what was the matter, and just how to mend it. Is that the window

that commands a magnificent prospect of Ponkwasset Mountain — in the advertisement?"

Maggie: "The very window!"

Leslie: "Does it condescend to overlook so
common a thing as the road up to the house?"

Maggie: "Of course; but why?"

Leslie, going to the open window, and stepping
through it upon the gallery, whither the other
young ladies follow her, and where her voice is
heard: "Yes, there they come! But I can't see
my young man. Is it possible that he's riding?
No, there he is! He was on the other side of
the stage. Don't you see him? Why he need n't
carry my hand-bag! He certainly might have let
that ride. I do wonder what he means by it! Or
is it only absent-mindedness? *Don't* let him see
us looking! It would be altogether too silly. *Do*
let's go in!"

Maggie, on their return to the parlor: "What
a great pity it is that he won't do! Is he handsome, Leslie? Why won't he do?"

Leslie: "You can tell in a moment, when you ve
seen him, Maggie. He's perfectly respectful and

nice, of course, but he's no more social perspective than — the man in the moon. He's never obtrusive, but·he's as free and equal as the Declaration of Independence; and when you did get up some little perspective with him, and tried to let him know, don't you know, that there was such a thing as a vanishing point somewhere, he was sure to do or say something so unconscious that away went your perspective — one simple crush."

Maggie: "How ridiculous!"

Leslie: "Yes. It was funny. But not just in that way. He isn't in the least common or uncouth. Nobody could say that. But he's going to be here two or three weeks, and it's impossible not to be civil; and it's very embarrassing, don't you see?"

Lilly: "Let me comfort you, Miss Bellingham. It will be the simplest thing in the world. We're all on the same level in the Ponkwasset Hotel. The landlord will bring him up during the evening and introduce him. Our table girls teach school in the winter and are as good as anybody. Mine calls me 'Lilly,' and I'm so small I can't help it.

They dress up in the afternoon, and play the piano. The cook's as affable, when you meet her in society, as can be."

Maggie: " Lilly ! "

Leslie, listening to Miss Roberts with whimsical trepidation: " Well, this certainly complicates matters.   But I think we shall be able to manage." At a sound of voices in the hall without, Miss Bellingham starts from her chair and runs to the corridor, where she is heard: " Thanks ever so much. So very good of you to take all this trouble.   Come into the parlor, mamma — there's nobody there but Maggie Wallace and Miss Roberts — and we 'll leave our things there till after tea."   She reënters the parlor with her mother and her aunt Kate, Mrs. Murray; after whom comes Stephen Blake with Leslie's bag in his hand, and the wraps of the other ladies over his arm.   His dress, which is evidently a prosperous fortuity of the clothing-store, takes character from his tall, sinewy frame ; a smile of somewhat humorous patience lights his black eyes and shapes his handsome moustache, as he waits in quiet self-possession the pleasure of the ladies.

III.

Mrs. Bellingham, Mrs. Murray, *and the* Young Girls.

Mrs. Bellingham, a matronly, middle-aged lady of comfortable, not cumbrous bulk, taking Miss Wallace by the hand and kissing her: "My dear child, how pleasant it is to see you so strong again! You 're a living testimony to the excellence of the air! How well you look!"

Leslie: "Mamma, — Miss Roberts." Mrs. Bellingham murmurously shakes hands with Miss Roberts, and after some kindly nods and smiles, and other shows of friendliness, provisionally and expectantly quiesces into a corner of the sofa, while her sister-in-law comes aggressively forward to assume the burden of conversation.

Mrs. Murray: "Well, a more fatiguing drive I certainly never knew! How do you do, Maggie?" She kisses Miss Wallace in a casual, unin-

2

terested way, and takes Lilly's hand. "Is n't this Miss Roberts? I am Mrs. Murray. I used to know your family — your uncle George, before that dreadful business of his. I believe it all came out right; he was n't to blame; but it was a shocking experience." Mrs. Murray turns from Lilly, and refers herself to the company in general: "It seems as if I should expire on the spot. I feel as if I had been packed away in my own hat-box for a week, and here, just as we arrive, the landlord informs us that he did n't expect us till tomorrow night, and he has n't an empty room in the house!"

Maggie: "No room! To-morrow night! What nonsense! Why it 's perfectly frantic! How could he have misunderstood? Why, it seems to me that I 've done *nothing* for a week past but tell him you were coming to-night!"

Mrs. Murray, sharply: "I have no doubt of it. But it does n't alter the state of the case. You may tell us to leave our things till *after tea,* Leslie. If they can't make up beds on the sofas and the piano, I don't know where we 're going to pass the night." In the moment of distressful sensation which follows Miss Wallace whispers something eagerly to her friend, Miss Roberts.

Maggie, with a laughing glance at Leslie and her mother, and then going on with her whispering: " Excuse the little confidence ! "

Mrs. Bellingham : " Conspiracy, I'm afraid. What are you plotting, Maggie ? "

Maggie, finishing her confidence : " Oh, we need n't make a mystery of such a little thing. We're going to offer you one of our rooms."

Mrs. Bellingham : "My dear, you are going to do nothing of the kind. We will never allow it."

Maggie : "Now, Mrs. Bellingham, you break my heart ! It's nothing, it's less than nothing. *I* believe we can make room for all three of you."

Mrs. Murray, promptly : " Let me go with you, young ladies. I'm an old housekeeper, and I can help you plan."

Maggie : "Oh do, Mrs. Murray. You can tell which room you'd better take, Lilly's or mine. Lilly's is " —

Mrs. Murray : " Oh ! I had forgotten that we

were detaining you!" Mrs. Murray is about to leave the room with the two young girls, when her eye falls upon Blake, who is still present, with his burden of hand-bags and shawls. "Leave the things on the table, please. We are obliged to you." Mrs. Murray speaks with a certain finality of manner and tone which there is no mistaking; Blake stares at her a moment, and then, without replying, lays down the things and turns to quit the room; at the same instant Leslie rises with a grand air from her mother's side, on the sofa, and sweeps towards him.

Leslie, very graciously: "Don't let our private afflictions drive you from a public room, Mr.—"

Blake : "Blake."

Leslie : "Mr. Blake. This is my mother, Mr. Blake, who wishes to thank you for all your kindness to us."

Mrs. Bellingham : "Yes, indeed, Mr. Blake, we are truly grateful to you."

Leslie, with increasing significance: "And my aunt, Mrs. Murray; and my friend, Miss Wallace; and Miss Roberts." Blake bows to each of the ladies as they are named, but persists in his movement to quit the room; Leslie impressively offers him her hand. "*Must* you go? Thank you, ever, ever so much!" She follows him to the door in his withdrawal, and then turns and confronts her aunt with an embattled front of defiance.

Maggie, with an effort breaking the embarrassing silence: "Come, Lilly. Let us go and take a look at our resources. We'll be back in a moment, Mrs. Bellingham."

IV.

Mrs. Bellingham *and* Leslie ; *afterwards* Mrs. Murray *and* Maggie.

Leslie, coming abruptly forward as her aunt goes out with the two young girls, and drooping meekly in front of her mother, who remains seated on the sofa : " Well, mamma ! "

Mrs. Bellingham, tranquilly contemplating her for a moment : " Well, Leslie ! " She pauses, and again silently regards her daughter. " Perhaps you may be said to have overdone it."

Leslie, passionately : " I can't help it, mother ! I could n't see him sent away in that insolent manner, I don't care who or what he is. Aunt Kate's tone was outrageous, atrocious, hideous ! And after accepting, yes, *demanding* every service he could possibly render, the whole afternoon ! It made me blush for her, and I was n't going to stand it."

Mrs. Bellingham : "If you mean by all that that your poor aunt is a very ungracious and exacting woman, I shall not dispute you. But she's your father's sister; and she's very much older than you. You seem to have forgotten, too, that your mother was present to do any justice that was needed. It's very unfortunate that he should have been able to do us so many favors, but that can't be helped now. It's one of the risks of coming to these out-of-the-way places, that you're so apt to be thrown in with nondescript people that you don't know how to get rid of afterwards. And now that he's been so cordially introduced to us all! Well, I hope you won't have to be crueller in the end, my dear, than your aunt meant to be in the beginning. So far, of course, he has behaved with perfect delicacy; but you must see yourself, Leslie, that even as a mere acquaintance he's quite out of the question; that however kind and thoughtful he's been, and no one could have been more so, he isn't a gentleman."

Leslie, impatiently : "Well, then, mother, I am! And so are you. And I think we are bound to

behave like gentlemen at any cost. I did n't mean
to ignore you. I did n't consider. I acted as I
thought Charley would have done."

Mrs. Bellingham: " Oh, my dear, my dear!
Don't you see there 's a very important difference?
Your brother is a man, and he can act without ref-
erence to consequences. But you are a young lady,
and you can't be as gentlemanly as you like without
being liable to misinterpretation. I shall expect
you to behave very discreetly indeed from this time
forth. We must consider now how our new friend
can be kindly, yet firmly and promptly, dropped."

Leslie: "Oh, it 's another of those embarrass-
ments that aunt Kate 's always getting me into! I
was discreet about it till she acted so horridly.
You can ask Maggie if I did n't talk in the wisest
way about it; like a perfect — owl. I saw it just
as you do, mamma, and I *was* going to drop him,
and so I will, yet; but I could n't see him so ungratefully trampled on. It 's *all* her doing! Who
wanted to come here to this out-of-the-way place?
Why, aunt Kate, — when I was eager to go to
Conway! I declare it 's too bad!"

Mrs. Bellingham : " That will do, Leslie."

Leslie : " And now she's gone off with those poor girls to crowd them out of house and home, I suppose. It's a shame! Why did you let her, mamma ? "

Mrs. Bellingham : " For the same reason that I let you talk on, my dear, when I've bidden you stop."

Leslie : " Oh, you dear, kind old mamma, you ! *You're* a gentleman, and you always were ! I only wish I could be half like you ! " She throws her arms round her mother's neck and kisses her. " I know you're right about this matter, but you must n't expect me to acknowledge that aunt Kate is. If you both said exactly the same thing, you would be right and she would be wrong, you'd say it so differently ! "

Mrs. Murray, who returns alone with signs of discontent and perplexity, and flings herself into a chair : " Their rooms are mere coops, and I don't see how even two of us are to squeeze into one of them. It's little better than impertinence to offer it to us. I've been down to see the landlord again, and you'll be pleased to know, Marion, that the only vacant room in the house had been engaged by the person to whom we've all just had the honor of an introduction." Leslie makes an impetuous movement, as if she were about to speak, but at a gesture from her mother she restrains herself, and Mrs. Murray continues: "Of course, if he had been a gentleman, in the lowest sense of the word, he would have offered his room to ladies who had none, at once. As long as he could make social capital out of his obtrusive services to us he was very profuse with them, but as soon as it came to a question of real self-sacrifice — to giving up his own ease and comfort for a single night"— A bell rings, and at the sound Mrs. Bellingham rises.

Mrs. Bellingham: "I suppose that's for supper. I think a cup of tea will put a cheerfuller face on our affairs. I don't at all agree with you about Mr. Blake's obligation to give up his room, nor about his services to us this afternoon; I'm sure common justice requires us to acknowledge that he was everything that was kind and thoughtful. Oh, you good child!"— as Miss Wallace appears at

the door, — "have you come to show us the way
to supper? Are you quite sure you've not gone
without tea on our account as well as given up
your room?" She puts her arm fondly round the
young girl's waist, and presses her cheek against
her own breast.

Maggie, with enthusiasm: Oh, Mrs. Bellingham,
you know I would n't ask anything better than to
starve on your account. I wish I *had n't* been
to tea! I'm afraid that you'll think the room
is a very slight offering when you come to see it
— it *is* such a little room; why, when I took Mrs.
Murray into it, it seemed all at once as if I saw it
through the wrong end of an opera-glass — it did
dwindle so!"

Leslie: "Never mind, Maggie; you're only too
good, as it is. If your room was an inch bigger,
we could n't bear it. I hope you may be without a
roof over your head yourself, some day! Can I
say anything handsomer than that? Don't wait
for me, mamma; I'll find the dining-room myself.
I'm rather too crumpled even for a houseless wan-
derer." She opens her bag where it stands on the

table. " I am going to make a flying toilet at one
of these glasses.   Do you think any one will come
in, Maggie ? "

Maggie : " There is n't the least danger.   This is
the parlor of the " transients," as they call them,
— the occasional guests, — and Lilly and I have it
mostly to ourselves when there are no transients.
The regular boarders stay in the lower parlor.
Shan't I help you, Leslie ? "

Leslie, rummaging through her bag : " No, indeed!   It 's only a question of brush and hair-pins.
Do go with mamma ! "   As Maggie obeys, Leslie
finds her brush, and going to one of the mirrors
touches the blonde masses of her hair, and then remains a moment, lightly turning her head from side
to side to get the effect.   She suddenly claps her
hand to one ear.   " Oh, horrors !   That ear-drop 's
gone again ! "   She runs to the table, reopens her
bag, and searches it in every part, talking rapidly
to herself.   " Well, really, it seems as if sorrows
would never end !   To think of that working out a
third time !   To think of my coming away without
getting the clasp fixed !   And to think of my not

leaving them in my trunk at the station! Oh dear me, I shall certainly go wild ! What *shall* I do? It is n't in the bag at all. It *must* be on the floor." Keeping her hand in helpless incredulity upon the ear from which the jewel is missing, she scrutinizes the matting far and near, with a countenance of acute anguish. Footsteps are heard approaching the door, where they hesitatingly arrest themselves. " Have you come back for me? Oh, I 've met with *such* a calamity! I 've lost one of my ear-rings. I could cry. Do come and help me mouse for it." There is no response to this invitation, and Leslie, lifting her eyes, in a little dismay confronts the silent intruder. " Mr. Blake ! "

V.

LESLIE *and* BLAKE.

Blake : " Excuse me. I expected to find your mother here. I did n't mean to disturb " —

Leslie, haughtily : " There 's no disturbance. It 's a public room : I had forgotten that. Mamma has gone to tea. I thought it was my friend Miss Wallace. I " — With a flash of indignation : " When you knew it was n't, why did you let me speak to you in that way ? "

Blake, with a smile : " I could n't know whom you took me for, and I had n't time to prevent your speaking."

Leslie : " You remained."

Blake, with a touch of resentment tempering his amusement : " I could n't go away after I had come without speaking to you. It was Mrs. Bellingham I was looking for. I 'm sorry not to find her, and I 'll go, now."

Leslie, hastily : " Oh no ! I beg your pardon. I did n't mean " —

Blake, advancing toward her, and stooping to pick up something from the floor, near the table : " Is this what you lost ? — if I 've a right to know that you lost anything."

Leslie : " Oh, my ear-ring ! Oh, thanks ! How did you see it ? I thought I had looked and felt everywhere." A quick color flies over her face as she takes the jewel from the palm of his hand. She turns to the mirror, and, seizing the tip of her delicate ear between the thumb and forefinger of one hand, hooks the pendant into place with the other, and then gives her head a little shake ; the young man lightly sighs. She turns toward him, with the warmth still lingering in her cheeks. " I 'm ever so much obliged to you, Mr. Blake. I wish I had your gift of doing all sorts of services — favors — to people. I wish I could find something for you."

Blake : " I wish you could — if it were the key to my room, which I came back in hopes of finding. I 've mislaid it somewhere, and I thought I might have put it down with your shawls here on the table." Leslie promptly lifts one of the shawls, and the key drops from it. "That's it. Miss Bellingham, I have a favor to ask: will you give this key to your mother?"

Leslie: "This key?"

Blake: "I have found a place to sleep at a farm-house just down the road, and I want your mother to take my room; I have n't looked into it yet, and I don't know that it's worth taking. But I suppose it's better than no room at all; and I know you have none."

Leslie, with cold hauteur, after looking absently at him for a moment: "Thanks. It's quite impossible. My mother would never consent."

Blake: "The room will stand empty, then. I meant to give it up from the first, — as soon as I found that you were not provided for, — but I hated to make a display of it before all the people down there in the office. I'll go now and leave the key with the landlord, as I ought to have done, without troubling you. But — I had hardly the chance of doing so after we came here."

Leslie, with enthusiasm: " Oh, Mr. Blake, do you really mean to give us your room after you 've been so odiously — Oh, it 's too bad ; it 's too bad ! You must n't ; no, you shall not."

Blake : " I will leave the key on the table here Good night. Or — I shall not see you in the morning : perhaps I had better say good-by."

Leslie : " Good-by ? In the morning ? "

Blake : " I 've changed my plans, and I 'm going away to-morrow. Good-by."

Leslie : " Going — Mamma will be very sorry to — Oh, Mr. Blake, I hope you are not going because — But indeed — I want you to believe " —

Blake, devoutly : " I believe it. Good-by ! " He turns away to go, and Leslie, standing bewildered and irresolute, lets him leave the room ; then she hastens to the door after him, and encounters her mother.

3 ·

VI.

Mrs. Bellingham *and* Leslie; *then* Mrs. Murray.

Mrs. Bellingham: "Well, Leslie. Are you quite ready? We went to look at Maggie's room before going down to tea. It's small, but we shall manage somehow. Come, dear. She's waiting for us at the head of the stairs. Why, Leslie!"

Leslie, touching her handkerchief to her eyes: "I was a little overwrought, mamma. I'm tired." After a moment: "Mamma, Mr. Blake" —

Mrs. Bellingham, with a look at her daughter: "I met him in the hall."

Leslie: "Yes, he has been here; and I thought I had lost one of my ear-rings; and of course he found it on the floor the instant he came in; and" —

Mrs. Murray, surging into the room, and going up to the table: "Well, Marion, the tea — What key is this? What in the world is Leslie crying about?"

Leslie, with supreme disregard of her aunt, and adamantine self-control: "Mr. Blake had come" — she hands the key to Mrs. Bellingham — "to offer you the key of his room. He asked me to give it."

Mrs. Bellingham: "The key of his room?"

Leslie: "He offers you his room; he had always meant to offer it."

Mrs. Bellingham, gravely: "Mr. Blake had no right to know that we had no room. It is too great a kindness. We can't accept it, Leslie. I hope you told him so, my dear."

Leslie: "Yes, mamma. But he said he was going to lodge at one of the farm-houses in the neighborhood, and the room would be vacant if you did n't take it. I could n't prevent his leaving the key."

Mrs. Bellingham: "That is all very well. But it does n't alter the case, as far as we are concerned. It is very good of Mr. Blake, but after what has occurred, it's simply impossible. We can't take it."

Mrs. Murray: "Occurred? Not take it? Of

course we will take it, Marion! I certainly am as-
tonished. The man will get a much better bed at
the farmer's than he's accustomed to. You talk
as if it were some act of self-sacrifice. I've no
doubt he's made the most of it. I've no doubt
he's given it an effect of heroism — or tried to.
But that you should fall in with his vulgar con-
ception of the affair, Marion, and Leslie should be
affected to tears by his magnanimity, is a little too
comical. One would think, really, that he had im-
periled life and limb on our account. All this sentiment about a room on the third floor! Give the
key to me, Marion." She possesses herself of it
from Mrs. Bellingham's passive hand. "Leslie will
wish to stay with you, so as to be near her young
friends. *I* will occupy this vacant room."

II.

"IN FAYRE FOREST."

I.

Two Tramps.

UNDER the shelter of some pines near a lonely by-road, in the neighborhood of the Ponkwasset Hotel, lie two tramps asleep. One of them, having made his bed of the pine-boughs, has pillowed his head upon the bundle he carries by day; the other is stretched, face downward, on the thick brown carpet of pine-needles. The sun, which strikes through the thin screen of the trees upon the bodies of the two men, is high in the heavens. The rattle of wheels is heard from time to time on the remoter highway; the harsh clatter of a kingfisher, poising over the water, comes from the direction of the river near at hand. A squirrel descends the trunk of an oak near the pines under which the men lie, and at sight of them stops, barks harshly, and then, as one of them stirs in his sleep, whisks back into the top of the oak. It is the luxurious tramp on the pine-boughs who stirs, and who alertly opens his eyes and sits up in his bed, as if the noisy rush of the squirrel had startled him from his sleep.

First Tramp, casting a malign glance at the top of the oak: "If I had a fair shot at you with this club, my fine fellow, I'd break you of that trick of waking people before the bell rings in the morning, and I'd give 'em broiled squirrel for breakfast when they did get up." He takes his bundle into his lap, and, tremulously untying it, reveals a motley heap of tatters; from these he searches out a flask, which he holds against the light, shakes at his ear, and inverts upon his lips. "Not a drop; not a square smell, even! I dreamt it." He lies down with a groan, and remains with his head pillowed in his hands. Presently he reaches for his stick, and again rising to a sitting posture strikes his sleeping comrade across the shoulders. "Get up!"

Second Tramp, who speaks with a slight brogue, briskly springing to his feet, and rubbing his shoul-ders: "And what for, my strange bedfellow?"

First Tramp: "For breakfast. What do people generally get up for in the morning?"

Second Tramp: "Upon my soul, I'd as soon have had mine in bed; I've a day of leisure before me. And let me say a word to you, my friend: the next time you see a gentleman dreaming of one of the most elegant repasts in the world, and just waiting for his stew to cool, don't you intrude upon him with that little stick of yours. I don't care for a stroke or two in sport, but when I think of the meal I've lost, I could find it in my heart to break your head for you, you ugly brute. Have you got anything to eat there in your wardrobe?"

First Tramp: "Not a crumb."

Second Tramp: "Or to drink?"

First Tramp: "Not a drop."

Second Tramp: "Or to smoke?"

First Tramp: "No."

Second Tramp: "Faith, you're nearer a broken head than ever, me friend. Wake a man out of a dream of that sort!"

First Tramp: "I've had enough of this. What do you intend to do?"

Second Tramp: "I'm going to assume the character of an impostor, and pretend at the next farm-house that I have n't had any breakfast, and have n't any money to buy one. It's a bare-faced deceit, I know, but" — looking down at his broken shoes and tattered clothes — "I flatter myself that I dress the part pretty well. To be sure, the women are not as ready to listen as they were once. The tramping-trade is overdone; there's too many in it; the ladies can't believe we're all destitute; it don't stand to reason."

First Tramp: "I'm tired of the whole thing."

Second Tramp: "I don't like it myself. But there's worse things. There's work, for example. By my soul, there's nothing disgusts me like these places where they tell you to go out and hoe potatoes, and your breakfast will be ready in an hour. I never could work with any more pleasure on an empty stomach than a full one. And the poor devils always think they've done something so fine when they say that, and the joke's so stale! I can tell them I'm not to be got rid of so easy. I'm not the lazy, dirty vagabond I look, at all;

I'm the inevitable result of the conflict between labor and capital; I'm the logical consequence of the prevailing corruption. I read it on the bit of newspaper they gave me round my dinner, yesterday; it was cold beef of a quality that you don't often find in the country."

First Tramp, sullenly: "I'm sick of the whole thing. I'm going out of it."

Second Tramp: "And what'll you do? Are ye going to work?"

First Tramp: "To work? No! To steal."

Second Tramp: "Faith, I don't call that going out of it, then. It's quite in the line of business. You're no bad dab at a hen-roost, now, as I know very well; and for any little thing that a gentleman can shove under his coat, while the lady of the house has her back turned buttering his lunch for him, I don't know the man I'd call master."

First Tramp: "If I could get a man to tell me the time of day by a watch I liked, I'd as lief knock him over as look at him."

Second Tramp: "Oh, if it's high-way robbery you mean, partner, I don't follow you."

First Tramp : " What 's the difference?"

Second Tramp : " Not much, if you take it one way, but a good deal if you take it another. It 's the difference between petty larceny and grand larceny ; it 's the difference between three months in the House of Correction and ten years in the State's Prison, if you 're caught, not to mention the risks of the profession."

First Tramp : " I 'd take the risks if I saw my chance." He lies down with his arms crossed under his head, and stares up into the pine. His comrade glances at him, and then moves stiffly out from the shelter of the trees, and, shading his eyes with one hand, peers down the road.

Second Tramp : " I did n't know but I might see your chance, partner. You would n't like an old gentleman with a load of potatoes to begin on, would ye? There 's one just gone up the cross-road. And yonder goes an umbrella-mender. I 'm afraid we shan't take any purses to speak of, in this neighborhood. Whoosh! Wait a bit — here 's somebody coming this way." The first tramp is sufficiently interested to sit up. " Faith, here 's your chance

at last, then, if you 're in earnest, my friend ; but it
stands six feet in its stockings, and it carries a stick
as well as a watch. I won't ask a share of the plun-
der, partner ; I 've rags enough of my own without
wanting to divide your property with the gentleman
coming." He goes back and lies down at the foot
of one of the trees, while the other, who has risen
from his pine-boughs, comes cautiously forward ;
after a glance at the approaching wayfarer he flings
away his cudgel, and, taking a pipe from his pocket
drops into a cringing attitude. The Irishman grins.
In another moment Blake appears from under the
cover of the woods and advances with long strides,
striking with his stick at the stones in the road as
he comes on, in an absent-minded fashion.

BLAKE *and the* TRAMPS.

First Tramp: "I say, mister!" Blake looks up, and his eye falls upon the squalid figure of the tramp; he stops. "Could n't you give a poor fellow a little tobacco for his pipe? A smoke comes good, if you don't happen to know where you 're going to get your breakfast."

Second Tramp, coming forward, with his pipe in his hand: "True for you, partner. A little tobacco in the hand is worth a deal of breakfast in the bush." Blake looks from one to the other, and then takes a paper of tobacco from his pocket and gives it to the first tramp, who helps himself and passes it to his comrade; the latter offers to return it after filling his pipe; Blake declines it with a wave of his hand, and walks on.

Second ˋTramp, calling after him: "God bless you! May you never want it!"

First Tramp : "Thank you, mister. *You're* a gentleman !"

Blake : "All right." He goes out of sight under the trees down the road, and then suddenly reappears and walks up to the two tramps, who remain where he left them and are feeling in their pockets for a match. "Did one of you call me a gentleman ?"

First Tramp : "Yes, I did, mister. No offense in that, I hope ?"

Blake : "No, but why did you do it ?"

First Tramp : "Well, you did n't ask us why we did n't go to work; and you did n't say that men who had n't any money to buy breakfast had better not smoke ; and you gave us this tobacco. I 'll call any man a gentleman that 'll do that."

Blake : "Oh, that's a gentleman, is it ? All right." He turns to go away, when the second tramp detains him.

Second Tramp : "Does your honor happen to have ever a match about you ?" Blake takes out his match-case and strikes a light. "God bless your honor. You 're a *real* gentleman."

Blake : " Then this makes me a gentleman past a doubt ? "

Second Tramp : " Sure, it does that."

Blake : " I 'm glad to have the matter settled." He walks on absently as before, and the tramps stand staring a moment in the direction in which he has gone.

Second Tramp, who goes back to the tree where he has been sitting and stretches himself out with his head on one arm for a quiet smoke : " That 's a queer genius. By my soul, I 'd like to take the road in *his* company. Sure, I think there is n't the woman alive would be out of cold victuals and old clothes when he put that handsome face of his in at the kitchen window."

First Tramp, looking down the road : " I wonder if that fellow could have a drop of spirits about him ! I say, mister ! " calling after Blake. " Hello, there, I say ! "

Second Tramp : " It 's too late, my worthy friend. · He 'll never hear you ; and it 's not likely he 'd come back to fill your flask for you, if he did. A gentleman of his character 'd think twice before he gave a tramp whiskey. Tobacco's another thing." He takes out the half-paper of tobacco, and looks at the label on it. "What an extravagant dog! It's the real cut-cavendish; and it smells as nice as it smokes. This luxury is what's destroying the country. 'With the present reckless expenditure in all classes of the population, and the prodigious influx of ignorant and degraded foreigners, there must be a constant increase of tramps.' True for you, Mr. Newspaper. 'T would have been an act of benevolence to take his watch from him, partner, and he never could tell how fast he was going to ruin. But you can't always befriend a man six feet high and wiry as a cat." He offers to put the tobacco into his pocket again, when his comrade slouches up, and makes a clutch at it.

First Tramp : " I want that."

Second Tramp : " Why, so ye do !"

First Tramp : " It's mine."

Second Tramp : " I'm keeping it for ye."

First Tramp : "I tell you the man gave it to me."

4

Second Tramp: " And he would n t take it back from me. Ah, will you, ye brute ? " The other seizes the wrist of the hand with which the Irishman holds the tobacco ; they wrestle together, when women's voices are heard at some distance down the road. " Whoosh ! Ladies coming." The first tramp listens, kneeling. The Irishman springs to his feet and thrusts the paper of tobacco into his pocket, and, coming quickly forward, looks down the road. " Fortune favors the brave, partner ! Here comes another opportunity — three of them, faith, and pretty ones at that ! Business before pleasure ; I 'll put off that beating again ; it 's all the better for keeping. Besides, it 's not the thing, quarreling before ladies." He is about to crouch down again at the foot of the tree as before, when his comrade hastily gathers up his bundle, and seizing him by the arm drags him back into the thicket behind the pine-trees. After a moment or two, three young ladies come sauntering slowly along the road.

III.

LESLIE, MAGGIE, *and* LILLY ; *then* LESLIE *alone.*

Lilly, delicately sniffing the air : " Fee, fi, fo, fum ; I smell the pipe of an Irishman."

Leslie : " Never! I know the flavor of refined tobacco, thanks to a smoking brother. Oh, what a lonely road!"

Lilly : " This loneliness is one of the charms of the Ponkwasset neighborhood. When you 're once out of sight of the hotel and the picnic-grounds you 'd think you were a thousand miles away from civilization. Not an empty sardine-box or a torn paper collar anywhere ! This scent of tobacco is an unheard-of intrusion."

Maggie, archly : " Perhaps Mr. Blake went this way. Does he smoke, Leslie ? "

Leslie, coldly : " How should I know, Maggie ? A gentleman would hardly smoke in ladies' com-

pany — strange ladies." She sinks down upon a
log at the wayside, and gazes slowly about with an
air of fastidious criticism that gradually changes to
a rapture of admiration. "Well, I certainly think
that, take it all in all, I never saw anything more
fascinating. It's wonderful! This little nook itself, with that brown carpet of needles under the
pines, and that heavy fringe of ferns there, behind
those trunks; and then those ghostly birches
stretching up and away, yonder — thousands of
them! How tall and slim and stylish they are.
And how they do march into the distance! I never
saw such multitudes; and their lovely paleness
makes them look as if one saw them by moonlight.
Oh, oh! How perfectly divine! If one could
only have their phantom-like procession painted!
But Corot himself could n't paint them. Oh, I
must make some sort of memorandum — I won't
have the presumption to call it a sketch." She
takes a sketch-book from under her arm, and lays
it on her knees, and then with her pencil nervously
traces on the air the lines of the distant birches.
"Yes; I *must.* I never shall see them so beauti-

ful again ! Just jot down a few lines, and wash in
the background when I get to the hotel. But
girls ; you must n't stay ! Go on and get the flow-
ers, and I 'll be done by the time you 're back. I
could n't bear to have you overlooking me; I 've
all the sensitiveness of a great artist. Do go !
But don't be gone long." She begins to work at
her sketch, without looking at them.

Maggie : " I 'm *so* glad, Leslie. I knew you 'd
be perfectly fascinated with this spot, and so I
did n't tell you about it. I wanted it to *burst* upon
you."

Leslie, with a little impatient surprise, as if she
had thought they were gone : "Yes, yes; never
mind. You did quite right. Don't stay long."
She continues to sketch, looking up now and then
at the scene before her ; but not glancing at her
companions, who walk away from her some paces,
when Miss Wallace comes back.

Maggie : " What time is it, Leslie ? Leslie ! "

Leslie, nervously : " *Oh !* What a start you gave
me." Glancing at her watch: " It 's nine minutes
past ten — I mean ten minutes past nine." Still
without looking at her: " Be back soon."

Maggie : "Oh, it is n't far. Again she turns away with Miss Roberts, but before they are quite out of sight Leslie springs to her feet and runs after them.

Leslie : " Oh, girls — girls ! "

Maggie, anxiously, starting back toward her: " What ? What ? "

Leslie, dreamily, as she returns to her place and sits down : " Oh, nothing. I just happened to think." She closes her eyes to a narrow line, and looks up at the birches. " There are so many horrid stories in the papers. But of course there can't be any in this out-of-the-way place, so far from the cities."

Maggie : " Any *what,* Leslie ? "

Leslie, remotely : " Tramps."

Maggie, scornfully : " There never was such a thing heard of in the whole region."

Leslie : " I thought not." She is again absorbed in study of the birches; and, after a moment of hesitation, the other two retreat down the road once more, lingering a little to look back in admiration of her picturesque devotion to art, and then

vanishing under the flickering light and shadow.
Leslie works diligently on, humming softly to herself, and pausing now and then to look at the
birches, for which object she rises at times, and,
gracefully bending from side to side, or stooping
forward to make sure of some effect that she has
too slightly glimpsed, resumes her seat and begins
anew. "No, that won't do!" — vigorously plying
her india-rubber on certain lines of the sketch.
"How stupid!" Then beginning to draw again,
and throwing back her head for the desired distance on her sketch: "Ah, that's more like. Still,
nobody could accuse it of slavish fidelity. Well!"
She sings: —

> " Through starry palm-roofs on Old Nile
>   The full-orbed moon looked clear;
> The bulbul sang to the crocodile,
>   ' Ah, why that bitter tear? '

> " ' With thy tender breast against the thorn,
>   Why that society-smile? '
> The bird was mute.   In silent scorn
> Slow winked the crocodile."

"How perfectly ridiculous! *Slow winked*" —

Miss Bellingham alternately applies pencil and rubber — "*slow winked the croco* — I never shall get that right; it's too bad! — *dile.*" While she continues to sketch, and sing *da capo*, the tramps creep stealthily from their covert. Apparently in accordance with some preconcerted plan, the surlier and huger ruffian goes down the road in the direction taken by Leslie's friends, and the Irishman stations himself unobserved at her side and supports himself with both hands resting upon the top of his stick, in an attitude of deferential patience and insinuating gallantry. She ceases singing and looks up.

IV.

The Young Girls *and the* Tramps.

Second Tramp: " Not to be interrupting you, miss," — Leslie stares at his grinning face in dumb and motionless horror, — " would ye tell a poor traveler the time of day, so that he need n't be eating his breakfast prematurely, if he happens to get any ? "

First Tramp, from his station down the road, in a hoarse undertone : " Snatch it out of her belt, you fool ! Snatch it ! He 's coming back. Quick ! " Leslie starts to her feet.

Second Tramp: " Ye see, miss, my friend 's impatient." Soothingly : " Just let me examine your watch. I give ye my honor I won't hurt you; don't lose your presence of mind, my dear; don't be frightened." As she shrinks back, he clutches at her watch-chain.

Leslie, in terror-stricken simplicity : "Oh, oh, no! Don't! Don't take my watch. My father gave it to me — and he 's dead."

Second Tramp : "Then he 'll never miss it, my dear. Don't oblige me to be rude to a lady. Give it here, at once, that 's a dear."

First Tramp : "Hurry, hurry! He 's coming!" As the Irishman seizes her by the wrist, Leslie utters one wild shriek after another, to which the other young girls respond, as they reappear under the trees down the road.

Maggie : " Leslie, Leslie! What is it? "

Lilly, at sight of Leslie struggling with the tramp: "Oh, help, help, help, somebody — do! "

Maggie : "Murder!"

First Tramp, rushing past them to the aid of his fellow: " Clap your hand over her mouth! Stop her noise, somehow! Choke her!" He springs forward, and while the Irishman stifles her cries with his hands, the other tears the watch-chain loose from its fastening. They suddenly release her, and as she reels gasping and swooning away, some one has the larger villain by the throat, who struggles with his assailant backward into the undergrowth, whence the crash of broken branches, with cries and curses, makes itself heard. Following this tumult comes the noise of a rush through the ferns, and then rapid footfalls, as of flight and pursuit on the hard road, that die away in the distance, while Maggie and Lilly hang over Leslie, striving to make out from her incoherent moans and laments what has happened.

Maggie: "Oh, Leslie, Leslie, Leslie, what was it? Do try to think! Do try to tell! Oh, I shall go wild if you don't tell what's the matter." ·

Leslie: "Oh, it was — Oh, oh, I feel as if I should never be clean again! How *can* I endure it? That filthy hand on my mouth! Their loathsome rags, their sickening faces! Ugh! Oh, I shall dream of it as long as I live! Why, why did I ever come to this horrid place?"

Maggie: "Leslie, — dear, good Leslie, — what was it all?"

Leslie, panting and sobbing: "Oh, two horrid, disgusting men! Don't ask me! And they told me to give them my watch, and I begged them not to take it. And one was a hideous little Irish wretch, and he kept running all round me, and oh, dear! the other was worse than he was; yes, worse! And he told him — oh, girls! — to choke me! And he came running up, and then the other put one of his hands over my mouth, and I could n't breathe; and I thought I should die; but I was n't going to let the wretches have my watch, if I could help it; and I kept struggling; and all at once they ran away, and " — putting her hand to her belt — " Oh, it 's gone, it 's gone, it 's gone! Oh, papa, papa! The watch you gave me is gone!" She crouches down upon the log, and leaning her head upon her hands against the trunk of a tree gives way to her tears and sobs, while the others kneel beside her in helpless distress. On this scene Blake emerges from the road down which the steps were heard. His face is pale, and he advances with his right arm held behind him, while the left clasps something which he extends as he speaks.

X.

Blake *and the* Young Girls.

Blake, after a pause in which he stands looking at Leslie unheeded by the others: "Here is your watch, Miss Bellingham."

Leslie, whirling swiftly round to her feet: "My watch? Oh, where did you find it?" She springs towards him and joyfully seizing it from his hand scans it eagerly, and then kisses it in a rapture. "Safe, safe, safe! Not hurt the least! My precious gift! Oh, how glad I am! It's even going yet! How did you get it? Where did you get it?"

Blake, who speaks with a certain painful effort while he moves slowly away backward from her: "I found it — I got it from the thief."

Leslie, looking confusedly at him: "How did you know they had it?"

Maggie: "Oh, it was you, Mr. Blake, who came flying past us, and drove them away! Did you have to fight them? Oh, did they hurt you?"

Leslie: "It was you — Why, how pale you look! There's blood on your face! Why, where were you? How did it all happen? It was you that drove them away? You? And I never thought of you! And I only thought about my-self—my watch! I never can forgive myself." She lets fall the watch from her heedless grasp, and he mechanically puts out the hand which he has been keeping behind him; she impetuously seizes it in her own and, suddenly shrinking, he subdues the groan that breaks from him to a sort of gasp and totters to the log where Leslie has been sitting.

Lilly: "Oh, see, Miss Bellingham; they've broken his wrist!"

Blake, panting: "It's nothing; don't—don't —"

Maggie: "Oh dear, he's going to faint! What *shall* we do if he does? I didn't know they *ever* fainted!" She wrings her hands in despair, while Leslie flings herself upon her knees at Blake's side.

"Ought n't we to support him, somehow? Oh yes do let 's support him, all of us!"

Leslie, imperiously: " Run down to the river as fast as ever you can, and wet your handkerchiefs to sprinkle his face with." She passes her arm round Blake's, and tenderly gathers his broken wrist into her right hand. "*One* can support him."

III.

A SLIGHT MISUNDERSTANDING.

MRS. MURRAY *and* MRS. BELLINGHAM.

THREE weeks after the events last represented Mrs. Bellingham and her sister-in-law are once more seated in the hotel parlor, both with sewing, to which the latter abandons herself with an apparently exasperated energy, while the former lets her work lie in her lap, and listens with some lady-like trepidation to what Mrs. Murray is saying.

Mrs. Murray : " From beginning to end it has been quite like a sensation play. Leslie must feel herself a heroine of melodrama. She is sojourning at a country inn, and she goes sketching in the woods, when two ruffians set upon her and try to rob her. Her screams reach the ear of the young man of humble life but noble heart, who professed to have gone away but who was still opportunely hanging about; he rushes on the scene and disperses the brigands, from whom he rends their prey. She seizes his hand to thank him for his sublime behavior, and discovers that his wrist has been broken by a blow from the bludgeon of one of the wicked ruffians. Very pretty, very charming, indeed; and so appropriate for a girl of Leslie's training, family, and station in life. Upon my word I congratulate you, Marion. To think of being the mother of a heroine! It was fortunate that you let her snub Mr. Dudley. If she had married him probably nothing of this kind would have happened."

Mrs. Bellingham, uneasily: "I ought to be glad the affair amuses you, but I don't see how even *you* can hold the child responsible for what has happened."

Mrs. Murray: "Responsible! I should be the last to do that, I hope. No, indeed. I consider her the victim of circumstances, and since the hero has been thrown back upon our hands, I'm sure every one must say that her devotion is most exemplary. I don't hold her responsible for that, even." As Mrs. Murray continues, Mrs. Bellingham's uneasiness increases, and she drops her hands with a baffled look upon the work in her lap. "It's quite *en règle* that she should be anxious about him; it would be altogether out of character, otherwise. It's a pity that he does n't lend himself more gracefully to being petted. When I saw her bringing him a pillow, that first day, after the doctor set his wrist and she had got him to repose his exhausted frame on the sofa, I was almost melted to tears. Of course it can end only in one way."

Mrs. Bellingham: "Kate, I will not have any more of this. It's intolerable, and you have no right to torment me so. You know that I'm as much vexed as you can be. It annoys me beyond endurance, but I don't see what, as a lady, I can do about it. Mr. Blake is here again by no fault of his own, certainly, and neither Leslie nor I can treat him with indifference."

Mrs. Murray: "I don't object to *your* treating him as kindly as you like, but you had better leave as little kindness as possible to Leslie. You must sooner or later recognize one thing, Marion, and take your measures accordingly. I advise you to do it sooner."

Mrs. Bellingham : " What do you mean ? "

Mrs. Murray: " I mean what you know well
enough : that Leslie is interested in this Mr. Blake.
I saw that she was, from the very first moment.
He 's just the kind of man to fascinate a girl like
Leslie ; you know that. He 's handsome, and he 's
shown himself brave ; and all that unconvention-
ality which marks him of a different class gives
him a charm to a girl's fancy, even when she has
recognized, herself, that he is n't a gentleman.
She soon forgets that, and sees merely that he is
clever and good. She would very promptly teach
a girl of his traditions her place, but a young man
is different."

Mrs. Bellingham : " I hope Leslie would treat
even a woman with consideration."

Mrs. Murray : " Oh, consideration, consideration !
You may thank yourself, Marion, and your impossible ideas, if this comes to the worst. You belong to one order of things or you belong to another. If you believe that several generations of
wealth, breeding, and station distinguish a girl so
that a new man, however good or wise he is, can

never be her equal, you must act on your belief, and in a case like this you can't act too promptly."

Mrs. Bellingham: "What should you do?"

Mrs. Murray: "Do? I should fling away all absurd ideas of consideration, to begin with. I should deal frankly with Leslie; I should appeal to her pride and her common sense; and I should speak so distinctly to this young man that he could n't possibly mistake my meaning. I should tell him — I should advise him to try change of air for his wound; or whatever it is."

Mrs. Bellingham, after a moment's dreary reflection: "That's quite impossible, Kate. I will speak to Leslie, but I can never offer offense to any one we owe so much."

Mrs. Murray: "Do you wish *me* to speak to him?"

Mrs. Bellingham: "No, I can't permit that, either."

Mrs. Murray: "Very well; then you must abide by the result." Mrs. Murray clutches her work together, stooping to recover dropping spools and scissors with an activity surprising in a lady of her massive person, and is about to leave the room, when the sound of steps and voices arrest her; a moment after Miss Bellingham and Blake, with his right arm in a sling, enter the room, so intent upon each other as not to observe the ladies in the corner.

II.

Leslie *and* Blake; Mrs. Murray *and* Mrs.
Bellingham *apart.*

Leslie: "I'm afraid you've let me tire you..
I'm such an insatiable walker, and I never thought
of your not being perfectly strong, yet."

Blake, laughing: "Why, Miss Bellingham, it
isn't one of my ankles that's broken."

Leslie, concessively: "No; but if you'd only
let me *do* something for you. I can both play and
sing, and really not at all badly. Shall I play to
you?" She goes up and strikes some chords on
the piano, and with her hand on the keys glances
with mock gravity round at Blake, who remains
undecided. She turns about. "Perhaps you'd
rather have me read to you?"

Blake: "Do you really wish me to choose?"

Leslie: "I do. And ask something difficult and
disagreeable."

Blake: "I'd rather have you talk to me than either."

Leslie: "Is that your idea of something difficult and disagreeable?"

Blake: I hope you won't find it so."

Leslie: "But I shan't feel that it's anything, then! Shall I begin to talk to you here? Or where?"

Blake: "This is a good place, but if I'm to choose again, I should say the gallery would be better."

Leslie: "Oh, you're choosing that because I said I wondered how people could come into the country and sit all their time in stuffy rooms!"

Blake, going to the window and looking out: "There are no seats." He returns, and putting the backs of two chairs together, lifts them with his left hand to carry them to the gallery.

Leslie, advancing tragically upon him and reproachfully possessing herself of the chairs: "Never! Do you think I have *no* sense of shame?" She lifts a chair in either hand and carries them out, while Blake in a charmed embarrassment follows her, and they are heard speaking without: "There! Or no! That's in a draught. You mustn't sit in a draught."

Blake: "It won't hurt me. I'm not a young lady."

Leslie: "That's the very reason it *will* hurt you. If you were a young lady you could stand anything. Anything you *liked*." There are indistinct murmurs of further feigned dispute, broken by more or less conscious laughter, to which Mrs. Bellingham listens with alarm and Mrs. Murray with the self-righteousness of those who have told you so, and who, having thus washed their hands of an affair, propose to give you a shower-bath of the water.

Mrs. Murray: "Well, Marion?"

Mrs. Bellingham, rising, with a heavy sigh: "Yes, it's quite as bad as you could wish."

Mrs. Murray: "As bad as *I* could wish? This is too much, Marion. What are you going to do?" Mrs. Bellingham is gathering up her work as if to quit the room, and Mrs. Murray's demand is pitched in a tone of falling indignation and rising amazement.

Mrs. Bellingham : "We can't remain to over-
hear their talk. I am going to my room."

Mrs. Murray : "Why, Marion, the child is your
own daughter!"

Mrs. Bellingham : "That is the very reason why
I don't wish to feel that she has cause to be
ashamed of me ; and I certainly should if I stayed
to eavesdrop."

Mrs. Murray : "How in the world should she
ever know it?"

Mrs. Bellingham : "I should tell her. But that
is n't the point, quite."

Mrs. Murray : "This is fantastic! Well, let her
marry her — Caliban! Why don't you go out and
join them? *That* need n't give her cause to blush
for you. Remember, Marion; that Leslie is an
ignorant, inexperienced child, and that it 's your
duty to save her from her silliness."

Mrs. Bellingham : "My daughter is a lady, and
will remember herself."

Mrs. Murray : "But she 's a woman, Marion,
and will forget herself!"

Mrs. Bellingham, who hesitates in a brief perplexity, but abruptly finishes her preparations for going out: " At any rate, I can't dog her steps, nor play the spy upon her. I wish to know only what she will freely tell me."

Mrs. Murray: " And are you actually going? Well, Marion, I suppose I must n't say what I think of you."

Mrs. Bellingham: " It is n't necessary that you should."

Mrs. Murray: " If I *were* to speak, I should say that your logic was worthy of Bedlam, and your morality of — of — the millenium!" She whirls furiously out of the parlor, and Mrs. Bellingham, with a lingering glance at the door opening upon the balcony, follows her amply eddying skirts. A moment after their disappearance, Leslie comes to the gallery door and looks exploringly into tho parlor.

III.

LESLIE *and* BLAKE ; *finally*, MRS. BELLINGHAM.

Leslie, speaking to Blake without : " I was sure I heard voices. But there's nobody." She turns, and glancing at the hills which show their irregular mass through the open window, sinks down into a chair beside the low gallery rail. " Ah, this is a better point still," and as Blake appears with his chair and plants it *vis-à-vis* with her : " Why *old* Ponkwasset, I wonder? But people always say *old* of mountains : old Wachusett, old Agamenticus, old Monadnock, old Ponkwasset. Perhaps the young mountains have gone West and settled down on the prairies, with all the other young people of the neighborhood. Would n't that explain it ? " She looks with openly-feigned seriousness at Blake, who supports in his left hand the elbow of his hurt arm. " I 'm sure it 's paining you."

Blake : " No, no; not the least. The fact is " — he laughs lightly — " I 'm afraid I was n't thinking about the mountains just now, when you spoke."

Leslie : " Oh, well, neither was I — very much." They both laugh. " But why do you put your hand under your arm, if it does n't pain you? "

Blake : " Oh ! — I happened to think of the scamp who broke it for me."

Leslie, shuddering : " Don't speak of it ! Or yes, do ! Tell me about it; I 've *wanted* to ask you. I ought to know about it; I hoped you would tell without asking. I can never be thankful enough that your walk happened to bring you back the same way. Why must you leave me to imagine all the rest ? "

Blake : Oh, those things are better imagined than described, Miss Bellingham."

Leslie : " But I want it described. I must hear it, no matter how terrible it is."

Blake : " It was n't terrible; there was very little of it, one way or the other. The big fellow would n't give up your watch; and I had to — urge him ; and the little Irishman came dancing up, and made a pass at us with his stick, and my wrist caught it. That's all."

Leslie, with effusion : " *All?* You risked your life to get me back my watch, and I asked about that first, and never mentioned you."

Blake : " I had n't done anything worth mentioning."

Leslie : " Then getting my watch was n't worth mentioning ! "

Blake : " Where is it ? I have n't seen you wear it."

Leslie : " I broke something in it when I threw it down. It does n't go. Besides, I thought perhaps you would n't like to see it."

Blake : " Oh, yes, I should."

Leslie, starting up : " I 'll go get it."

Blake : " Not now ! " They are both silent. Leslie falters and then sits down again, and folds one hand over the other on the balcony rail, letting her fan dangle idly by its chain from her waist. He leans forward a little, and taking the fan, opens and shuts it, while she looks down upon him with a slight smile ; he relinquishes it with a glance at her, and leans back again in his chair.

Leslie : "Well, what were you thinking about that hideous little wretch who hurt you ?".

Blake : "Why, I was thinking, for one thing, that he did n't mean to do it."

Leslie : "Oh! Why *did* he do it, then ?"

Blake : "I believe he meant to hit his partner, though I can 't exactly say why. It went through my mind. And I was thinking that a good deal might be said for tramps."

Leslie : "For tramps that steal watches and break wrists? My philanthropy does n't rise to those giddy heights, quite. No decidedly, Mr. Blake, I draw the line at tramps. They never look clean, and why don't they go to work ?"

Blake : "Well they could n't find work just now, if they wanted it, and generally I suppose they don't want it. A man who 's been out of work three months is glad to get it, but if he 's idle a year he does n't want it. When I see one of your big cotton mills standing idle, I know that it means just so much tramping, so much starving and stealing, so much misery and murder. We 're all part

6

of the tangle ; we 're all of us to blame, we 're none
of us to blame."

Leslie : "Oh, that 's very well. But if you pity
such wretches, what becomes of the *deserving*
poor ? "

Blake : "I 'm not sure there are any deserving
poor, as you call them, any more than there are deserving rich. So I don't draw the line at tramps.
The fact is, Miss Bellingham, I had just been doing
those fellows a charity before they attacked you, —
given them some tobacco. You don't approve of
that ? "

Leslie : " Oh, I like smoking ! "

Blake, laughing: "And I got their idea of a
gentleman."

Leslie, after a moment : "Yes ? What was that ? "

Blake : " A man who gives you tobacco, and
does n't ask you why you don't go to work. A
real gentleman has matches about him to light your
pipe with afterwards. Is that your notion of a
gentleman ? "

Leslie, consciously : " I don't know ; not exactly."

Blake : " It made me think of the notion of a

gentleman I once heard from a very nice fellow years ago : he believed that you could n't be a gentleman unless you began with your grandfather. I was younger then, and I remember shivering over it, for it left *me* quite out in the cold, though I could n't help liking the man ; he was a gentleman in spite of what he said, — a splendid fellow, if you made allowance for him. You have to make allowances for everybody, especially for men who have had all the advantages. It 's apt to put them wrong for life ; they get to thinking that the start is the race. I used to look down on that sort of men, once — in theory. But what I saw of them in the war taught me better ; they only wanted an emergency, and they could show themselves as good as anybody. It is n't safe to judge people by their circumstances ; besides, I 've known too many men who had all the *dis*advantage and never came to anything. Still I prefer the tramp's idea — perhaps because it 's more flattering — that you are a gentleman if you choose to be so. What do you think ? "

Leslie : " I don't know." After an interval long

enough to vanquish and banish a disagreeable con-
sciousness: " I think it's a very unpleasant subject.   Why don't you talk of something else ? "

Blake : " Oh, I was n't to talk at all, as I understood.   I was to be talked to."

Leslie : " Well, what shall I talk to you about?
You must choose that, too."

Blake : " Let us talk about yourself, then.·'

Leslie : " There *is* nothing about me.   I 'm just
like every other girl.   Get Miss Wallace to tell
you about herself, some day, and then you 'll know
my whole history.   I 've done everything that
she 's done.   We had the same dancing, singing,
piano, French, German, and Italian lessons ; we
went to the same schools and the same lectures ;
we have both been abroad, and can sketch, and
paint on tiles.   We 're as nearly alike as the same
experiences and associations could make us, and
we 're just like all the other girls we know.   Is n't
it rather monotonous ? "

Blake : " I don't know all the other girls that
you know.   If I can judge from Miss Wallace, I
don't believe you 're like them ; but they may be
like you."

Leslie, laughing : " That 's too fine a distinction for me. And you have n't answered my question."

Blake, gravely: " No, it is n't monotonous to me; it 's all very good, I think. I 'm rather old-fashioned about women ; I like everything in their lives to be regular and ordered by old usage."

Leslie : " Then you don't approve of originality ? "

Blake : " I don't like eccentricity."

Leslie : " Oh, I do. I should like to do all sorts of odd things, if I dared."

Blake : " Well, your not daring is a great point. If I had a sister, I should want her to be like all the other girls that are like you."

Leslie : " You compliment ! She could n't be like me."

Blake : " Why ? "

Leslie : " Why ? Oh, I don't know." She hesitates, and then with a quick glance at him : " She would have dark eyes and hair, for one thing." They both laugh.

Blake : " Was that what you meant to say ? "

Leslie : " Is n't it enough to say what you mean, without being obliged to say what you meant ? "

Blake: " Half a loaf is better than no bread ; beggars must n't be choosers."

Leslie: " Oh, if you put it so meekly as that you humiliate me. I must tell you now: I meant a question."

Blake: " What is it ? "

Leslie: " But I can't ask it, yet. Not till I 've got rid of some part of my obligations."

Blake: " I suppose you mean what I — what happened."

Leslie: " Yes."

Blake: "I 'm sorry that it happened, then; and I had been feeling rather glad of it, on the whole. I shall hate it if it 's an annoyance to you."

Leslie: " Oh, — not annoyance, exactly."

Blake: " What then ? Should you like a receipt in full for all gratitude due me ? "

Leslie: " I should like to feel that we had done something for you in return."

Blake: " You can cancel it all by giving me leave to enjoy being just what and where I am."

Leslie, demurely, after a little pause: " Is a broken wrist such a pleasure, then ? "

Blake: "I take the broken wrist for what it brings. If it were not for that I should be in New York breaking my heart over some people I'm connected with in business there, and wondering how to push a little invention of mine without their help. Instead of that"—

Leslie, hastily: "Oh! Invention? Are you an inventor, too, Mr. Blake? Do tell me what it is."

Blake: "It's an improved locomotive driving-wheel. But you'd better let me alone about that, Miss Bellingham; I never stop when I get on my driving-wheel. That's what makes my friends doubtful about it; they don't see how any brake can check it. They say the Westinghouse air-brake would exhaust the atmosphere of the planet on it without the slightest effect. You see I *am* rather sanguine about it." He laughs nervously.

Leslie: "But what have those New York people to do with it?"

Blake : "Nothing, at present. That's the worst of it. They were partners of mine, and they got me to come on all the way from Omaha, and then I found out that they had no means to get the thing going."

Leslie: "Oh! How could they do it?"

Blake: "Well, I used language to that effect myself, but they did n't seem to know; and I ran up here to cool off and think the matter over for a fresh start. You see, if I succeed it will be an everlasting fortune to me; and if I fail, — well, it will be an everlasting *mis*fortune. But I 'm not going to fail. There; I 'm started! If I went on a moment longer, no power on earth could stop me. I suppose your 're not much used to talking about driving-wheels, Miss Bellingham?"

Leslie: "We don't *often* speak of them. But they must be very interesting to those that understand them."

Blake: "I can't honestly say they are. They 're like railroads; they 're good to get you there."

Leslie: "Where?"

Blake: "Well, in my case, away from a good deal of drudgery I don't like, and a life I don't altogether fancy, and a kind of world I know too well. I should go to Europe, I suppose, if the wheel succeeded. I 've a curiosity to see what the apple is like on the other side; whether it 's riper or only rottener. And I always believed I should quiet down somewhere, and read all the books I wanted to, and make up for lost time in several ways. I don't think I should look at any sort of machine for a year."

Leslie, earnestly: "And would all that happen if you had the money to get the driving-wheel going?"

Blake, with a smile at her earnestness: "I'm not such a driving-wheel fanatic as that. The thing has to be fully tested, and even after it's tested, the roads may refuse to take hold of it."

Leslie, confidently: "They can't — when they see that it's better."

Blake: "I wish I could think so. But roads are human, Miss Bellingham. They prefer a thing that's just as well to something that's much better — if it costs much to change."

Leslie: "Well, then, if you don't believe the roads will take hold of it, why do you want to test it? Why don't you give it up at once?"

Blake: "It won't give me up. I do believe in it, you know, and I can't stop where I am with it. I must go on."

Leslie : "Yes. I should do just the same. I should never, *never* give it up. I know you'll be helped. Mr. Blake, if this wheel"—

Blake : "Really, Miss Bellingham, I feel ashamed for letting you bother yourself so long with that ridiculous wheel. But you wouldn't stick to the subject: we were talking about you."

Leslie, dreamily: "About me?" Then abruptly: "Mamma will wonder what in the world has become of me." She rises, and Blake, with an air of slight surprise, follows her example. She leads the way into the parlor, and lingeringly drawing near the piano, she strikes some chords, and as she stands over the instrument, she carelessly plays an air with one hand. Then, without looking up: "Was that the air you were trying to remember?"

Blake, joyfully: "Oh yes, that's it; that's it, at last!"

Leslie, seating herself at the piano and running over the keys again: "I think I can play it for you; it's rather old-fashioned, now." She plays and sings, and then rests with her hands on the keys, looking up at Blake where he stands leaning one elbow on the corner of the piano.

Blake: " I 'm very much obliged."

Leslie, laughing : " And I 'm very much surprised."

Blake: " Why ? "

Leslie: " I should think the inventor of a driving-wheel would want something a great deal more stirring than this German sentimentality and those languid, melancholy things from Tennyson that you liked."

Blake: " Ah, that 's just what I don't want. I 've got stir enough of my own."

Leslie: " I wish I could understand you."

Blake: " Am I such a puzzle ? I always thought myself a very simple affair."

Leslie: " That 's the difficulty. I wish "—

Blake : " What ? "

Leslie: " That I could say something wrong in just the right way ! "

Blake, laughing : " How do you know it 's wrong ? "

Leslie: " It is n't, if you don't think so."

Blake: " I don't, so far."

Leslie: "Ah, don't joke. It's a very serious matter."

Blake: "Why should I think it was wrong?"

Leslie: "I don't know that you will. Mr. Blake" —

Blake: " Well?"

Leslie: "Did you know— If I begin to say something, and feel like stopping before I've said it, you won't ask questions to make me go on?" Very seriously.

Blake, with a smile of joyous amusement, looking down at her as he lounges at the corner of the piano: "I won't even ask you to begin." Leslie passes her hand over the edges of the keys, without making them sound; then she drops it into her lap and there clasps it with the other hand, and looks up at Blake.

Leslie: "Did you know I was rich, Mr. Blake?"

Blake: "No, Miss Bellingham, I did n't." His smile changes from amusement to surprise, and he colors faintly.

Leslie, blushing violently: "Well, I am, — if being rich is having a great deal more money to do what you please than you know what to do with." Blake listens with a look of deepening mystification; she hurries desperately on: "I have this money in my own right; it's what my uncle left me, and I can give it all away if I choose." She pauses again, as if waiting for Blake to ask her to go on, but he remains loyally silent; his smile has died away, and an embarrassment increases upon both of them. She looks up at him again, and implores: "What *will* you think of what I'm going to say?"

Blake, breaking into a troubled laugh: "I can't imagine what you're going to say."

Leslie: "Don't laugh! I know you won't — O Mr. Blake, you said you liked girls to be just like everybody else, and old-established, and that; and I know this is as eccentric as it can be. It is n't at all the thing, I know, for a young lady to say to a gentleman; but you're not like the others, and — Oh, it does n't seem possible that I should have begun it! It seems perfectly monstrous!

But I know you won't misinterpret; I must, I must go on, and the bluntest and straightforwardest way will be the best way." She keeps wistfully scanning Blake's face as she speaks, but apparently gathers no courage or comfort from it. "Mr. Blake!"

Blake, passively: "Well?"

Leslie, with desperate vehemence: "I want — Oh, what will you think of me! But no, you're too good yourself not to see it in just the right way. I'm sure that you won't think it — unladylike — for me to propose such a thing, merely because — because most people wouldn't do it; but I shall respect your reasons — I shall know you're right — even if you refuse me; and — O Mr. Blake, I want to go into partnership with you!"

Blake, recoiling a pace or two from the corner of the piano, as Leslie rises from the stool and stands confronting him; "To — to — go into" —

Leslie: "Yes, yes! But how dreadfully you take it; and you promised — Oh, I *knew* you wouldn't like it! I know it seems dreadfully queer, and not at all delicate. But I thought — I thought — from what you said — You said those people had no money to push your invention, and here I have all this money doing nobody any good — and you 've done nothing but heap one kindness after another on us — and why *should n't* you take it, as much as you want, and use it to perfect your driving-wheel? I 'm sure I believe in it; and " — She has followed him the pace or two of his withdrawal; but now, at some changing expression of his face, she hesitates, falters, and remains silent and motionless, as if fixed and stricken mute by the sight of some hideous apparition. Then with a wild incredulity: "Oh!" and indignation, "Oh!" and passionate reproach and disappointment, "Oh! How cruel, how shameless, how horrid!" She drops her face into her hands, and sinks upon the piano-stool, throwing her burdened arms upon the keys with a melodious crash.

Blake: "Don't, don't! For pity's sake, don't, my — Miss Bellingham!" He stands over her in helpless misery and abject self-reproach. "Good heavens, I did n't — It was all " —

Leslie, springing erect: "Don't speak to me.

Your presence, your being alive in the same world after that is an insufferable insult! For you to dare! Ah! No woman could say what you thought. No lady " —

Blake : " Wait ! " He turns pale, and speaks low and steadily : " You must listen to me now ; you must hear what I never dreamt I should dare to say. I loved you! If that had not bewildered me I could not have thought — what was impossible. It was a delusion dearer than life ; but I was ashamed of the hope it gave me even while it lasted. Don't mistake *me*, Miss Bellingham ; I could have died to win your love, but if your words had said what they seemed to say, I would not have taken what they seemed to offer. But that's past. And now that I have to answer your meaning, I must do it without thanks. You place me in the position of having told my story to hint for your help " —

Leslie, in vehement protest : " Oh, no, no, no ! I never dreamt of such a thing ! I could n't ! "

Blake : " Thank you at least for that ; and — Good-by ! " He bows and moves away toward the door.

Leslie, wildly : "Oh, don't go, don't go! What have I done, what shall I do ?"

Blake, pausing, and then going abruptly back to her : "You can forgive me, Miss Bellingham ; and let everything be as it was."

Leslie, after a moment of silent anguish : "No, no. That's impossible. It can never be the same again. It must all end. I can forgive you easily enough ; it was nothing ; the wrong was all mine. I've been cruelly to blame, letting you — go on. Oh, yes, very, very much. But I did n't know it ; and I did n't mean anything by anything. No, I could n't. Good-by. You are right to go. You must n't see me any more. I shall never forget your goodness and patience." Eagerly : "You would n't want me to forget it, would you ? "

Blake, brokenly : "Whatever you do will be right. God bless you, and good-by." He takes up her right hand in his left, and raises it to his lips, she trembling, and as he stands holding it Mrs. Bellingham enters with an open letter.

Mrs. Bellingham : "Leslie"—

Leslie, who withdraws her hand, and after a mo-

7

mentary suspense turns unashamed to her mother : " Mr. Blake is going away, mamma " — Mrs. Bellingham faintly acknowledges his parting bow. Leslie watches him go, and then turns away with a suppressed sob.

IV.

MRS. MURRAY'S TRIUMPH.

I.

Mrs. Bellingham *and* Leslie.

Leslie: " Well, mamma, what will you say to me now?" Without the inspiration of Blake's presence, she stands drearily confronting her mother in Mrs. Bellingham's own room, where the latter, seated in her easy-chair, looks up into Leslie's face.

Mrs. Bellingham: " Nothing, Leslie. I am waiting for you to speak."

Leslie: " Oh, I can't speak unless you ask me." She drops into a chair, and hiding her face in her handkerchief weeps silently. Her mother waits till her passion is spent and she has wiped her tears, and sits mutely staring toward the window.

Mrs. Bellingham: "Is he coming back again, Leslie?"

Leslie: "No."

Mrs. Bellingham: " Was it necessary that you should let him take leave of you in that way?"

Leslie, sighing: "No, it was n't necessary. But — it was inevitable."

Mrs. Bellingham: "What had made it inevitable? Remember, Leslie, that you asked me to question you."

Leslie: "I know it, mamma."

Mrs. Bellingham: "And you need n't answer if you don't like."

Leslie: "I don't like, but I will answer, all the same, for you have a right to know. I had been saying something silly to him."

Mrs. Bellingham, with patient hopelessness: "Yes?"

Leslie: "It seems so, now; but I know that I spoke from a right motive, — a motive that you would n't disapprove of yourself, mamma."

Mrs. Bellingham: "I 'm sure of that, my dear."

Leslie: "Well, you see — Could n't you go on and ask me, mamma?"

Mrs. Bellingham: "I don't know what to ask, Leslie."

Leslie: "It 's so hard to tell, without!" Desperately: "Why, you see, mamma, Mr. Blake had

told me about a thing he had been inventing, and
how some people in New York had promised him
money to get it along, — push it, he said, — and
when he came on all the way from Omaha, he
found that they had no money; and so — and so —
I — I offered him some."

Mrs. Bellingham: "Oh, Leslie!"

Leslie: "Yes, yes, it seems horrid, now, — perfectly hideous. But I did so long to do something
for him because he had done so much for us, and I
think he is so modest and noble, and I felt so sorry
that he should have been so cruelly deceived.
Was n't that a good motive, mamma?"

Mrs. Bellingham: "Oh, yes, my poor headlong
child! But what a thing for a young lady to propose! I can't imagine how you could approach the
matter."

Leslie: "That 's the worst of it, — the very
worst. Of course, I never *could* have approached
such a thing with any other young man; but I
thought there was such a difference between us,
don't you know, in everything, that it would be
safe; and I thought it would be better — he would

like it better — if there was no beating about the bush ; and so I said — I said — that I wanted to go into partnership with him."

Mrs. Bellingham, with great trouble in her voice, but steadily : " What answer did he make you, Leslie ? "

Leslie : " Oh, I was justly punished for looking down upon him. At first he blushed in a strange sort of way, and then he turned pale and looked grieved and angry, and at last repeated my words in a kind of daze, and I blundered on, and all at once — I saw what he thought I had meant ; he thought — Oh dear, dear, — he thought " — she hides her face again, and sobs out the words behind her handkerchief — " that I w-w-anted to — to — to marry him ! Oh, how shall I ever endure it ? It was a thousand times worse than the tramps, — a thousand times." Mrs. Bellingham remains silently regarding her daughter, who continues to bemoan herself, and then lifts her tear-stained face : " Don't you think it was ungratefully, horridly, cruelly vulgar ? "

Mrs. Bellingham : " Mr. Blake can't have the

rcfinement of feeling that you've been used to in
the gentlemen of your acquaintance; I'm glad that
you've found that out for yourself, though you've
had to reach it through such a bitter mortifica-
tion. If such a man misunderstood you" —

Leslie, indignantly: " Mr. Blake is quite as good
as the gentlemen of my acquaintance, mamma; he
could n't help thinking what he did, I blundered
so, and when I flew out at him, and upbraided
him for his — ungenerosity, and hurt his feelings
all I could, he excused himself in a perfectly satisfactory way. He said" —

Mrs. Bellingham : " What, Leslie ? "

Leslie, with a drooping head: " He said — he
used words more refined and considerate than I
ever dreamt of — he said he was always thinking
of me in that way without knowing it, and hoping
against hope, or he could never have misunderstood
me in the world. And then he let me know that
he would n't have taken me, no matter how much
he liked me, if what he thought for only an instant
had been true; and he could never have taken my
money, for that would have made him seem like

begging, by what he had told me. And he talked splendidly, mamma, and he put me down, as I deserved, and he was going away, and I called him back, and we agreed that we must never see each other again; and — and I could n't help his kissing my hand." She puts up her handkerchief and sobs, and there is an interval before her mother speaks in a tone of compassion, yet of relief.

Mrs. Bellingham: " Well, Leslie, I 'm glad that you could agree upon so wise a course. This has all been a terribly perplexing and painful affair ; and I have had my fears, my dear, that perhaps it had gone so far with you that " —

Leslie, vehemently : " Why, so it had ! I did n't know I liked him so, but I do ; and I give him up — I gave him up — because you all hate him, yes, *all ;* and you shut your eyes, and *won't* see how kind and brave and good he is ; and I can't hold out against you. Yes, he must go ; but he takes my broken heart with him."

Mrs. Bellingham, sternly: " Leslie, this is absurd. You know yourself that he 's out of the question."

Leslie, flinging herself down and laying her head in her mother's lap with a desolate cry: "O mamma, mamma, don't speak so harshly to me, or I shall die. I *know* he's out of the question; yes, yes, I do. But how? How, mamma? How is he out of the question? That's what I can't understand!"

Mrs. Bellingham: "Why, to begin with, we know nothing about him, Leslie."

Leslie, eagerly: "Oh yes, I do. He's told me all about himself. He's an inventor. He's a genius. Yes, he knows everything, indeed he does; and in the war he was an engineer. If you could only hear him talk as I do" —

Mrs. Bellingham: "I dare say. But even a civil engineer" —

Leslie: "A *civil* engineer! I should hope *not.* I should be ashamed of a man who had been a civilian during the war. He always had this great taste for mechanics, and he studied the business of a machinist — I don't know what it is, exactly; but he knows all about steam, and he can build a whole engine, himself; and he happened to be a private soldier going somewhere on a Mississippi gunboat when the engineer was killed, and he took charge of the engine at once, and was in the great battles with the boat afterwards. He's a military engineer."

Mrs. Bellingham: "He's a *steamboat* engineer, Leslie."

Leslie: "He was an officer of the boat — an officer" —

Mrs. Bellingham, with a groan: "Oh, he wasn't an officer of the sort you think; he had no military rank; he had the place of a clever artisan."

Leslie: "I don't understand."

Mrs. Bellingham: "He looked after the machinery, and saw that the boiler didn't burst, — I don't know what. But you might as well marry a locomotive-driver, as far as profession goes."

Leslie, aghast: "Do you mean that when Mr. Blake was an engineer, he didn't wear any coat, and had his sleeves rolled up, and went about with a stringy wad of oily cotton in his hand?"

Mrs. Bellingham: "Yes."

Leslie: "Oh!" She excludes the horrible vision by clasping both hands over her eyes.

Mrs. Bellingham, very gravely: "Now listen to me, Leslie. You know that I am not like your aunt Kate,— that I never talk in that vulgar way about classes and stations, don't you?"

Leslie, still in a helpless daze: "Oh, yes, mamma. I've always been a great deal worse than you, myself."

Mrs. Bellingham: "Well, my dear, then I hope that you will acquit me of anything low or snobbish in what I have to say. There is a fitness in all things, and I speak out of respect to that. It is simply impossible that a girl of your breeding and ideas and associations should marry a man of his. Recollect that no one belongs entirely to themselves. You are part of the circle in which you have always moved, and he is part of the circumstances of his life. Do you see?"

Leslie: "Yes." She lapses from a kneeling to a crouching posture, and resting one elbow on her mother's knee poises her chin on her hand, and listens drearily.

Mrs. Bellingham: "We may say that it is no matter what a man has been; that we are only

concerned with what Mr. Blake is now. But
the trouble is that every one of us is what they
have been. If Mr. Blake's early associations have
been rude and his business coarse, you may be
sure they have left their mark upon him, no matter how good he may be naturally. I think he is
of a very high and sweet nature ; he seems so " —

Leslie : " Oh, he is, he is ! "

Mrs. Bellingham : " But he can't outlive his own
life. Is n't that reasonable ? "

Leslie, hopelessly : " Yes, it seems so."

Mrs. Bellingham : " You can't safely marry any
man whose history you despise. Marriage is a terrible thing, my dear ; young girls can never understand how it searches out the heart and tries and
tests in every way. You must n't have a husband
whom you can imagine with a wad of greasy cotton in his hand. There will be wicked moments
in which you will taunt and torment each other."

Leslie : " O mamma, mamma ! "

Mrs. Bellingham : " Yes, it is so ! The truest
love can come to that. And in those moments it
is better that all your past and present should be

of the same level as his ; for you would n't hesitate to throw any scorn in his teeth ; you would be mad, and you must not have deadly weapons within reach. I speak very plainly."

Leslie: " Terribly ! "

Mrs. Bellingham: " But that is the worst. There are a thousand lighter trials, which you must meet. Where would you live, if you married him ? You have a fortune, and you might go to Europe " —

Leslie: " I *never* would sneak away to Europe with him ! "

Mrs. Bellingham: " I should hope not. But if you remained at home, how would you introduce him to your friends ? Invention is n't a profession ; would you tell them that he was a machinist or a steamboat engineer by trade ? And if they found it out without your telling ? "

Leslie, evasively : " There are plenty of girls who marry men of genius, and it does n't matter what the men have done, — how humble they have been. If they 're geniuses " —

Mrs. Bellingham: " O Leslie, such men have won all the honors and distinctions before they

marry. Girls like you, my dear, don't marry geniuses in their poverty and obscurity. Those men
spend years and years of toil and study, and strug-
gle through a thousand difficulties and privations,
and set the world talking about them, before they
can even be asked to meet the ordinary people of
our set in society. Wait till Mr. Blake has
shown " —

Leslie : " But he 'd be an old man by that time,
and then I should n't want him. If I know *now*
that he 's going to be great " —

Mrs. Bellingham : " My dear, you know nothing
whatever about him, except that his past life has
been shabby and common."

Leslie, with sudden spirit : " Well, then, mamma,
at least I don't know anything horrid of him, as
some girls must know of the young men they
marry, — and the old men, too. Just think of Vi-
olet Emmons's match with that count, there in
Paris ! And Aggy Lawson's, with that dreadful
old Mr. Lancaster, that everybody says has been
so wicked ! I 'd rather marry Mr. Blake, a thousand times, if he had been a — I don't know
what ! "

Mrs. Bellingham: " You have no right to take things at their worst, Leslie. Remember all the girls you know, and the accomplished men they have married in their own set; men who are quite their equals in goodness as well as station and wealth and breeding. That's what I want you to do."

Leslie: " Do you wish me to marry somebody I don't like?"

Mrs. Bellingham: " Be fair, Leslie. I merely wish you to like somebody you ought to marry, — when the proper time comes. How do you know that Mr. Blake isn't quite as bad as the count or Mr. Lancaster?"

Leslie, with a burst of tears: " Oh, mamma, you just now said yourself that you believed he was good and sweet, and you have seen the beautiful delicacy he behaves towards women with. Well, well," —she rises, and catches in her hand a long coil of her hair which has come loose from the mass, and stands holding it while she turns tragically toward her mother, — " let it all go. I will never marry at all, and then at least I can't displease you. I give him up, and I hope it will make you happy, mamma."

Mrs. Bellingham, rising: "Leslie, is this the way you reward my anxiety and patience? I have reasoned with you as a woman of sense, and the return you make is to behave as a petulant child. I will never try to control you in such a matter as this, but you know now what I think, and you can have your own way if you like it better or believe it is wiser than mine. Oh, my poor child!" — clasping Leslie's head between her hands and tenderly kissing the girl's hair, — "don't you suppose your mother's heart aches for you? Marry him if you will, Leslie, and I shall always love you. I hope I may never have to pity you more than I do now. All that I ask of you, after all, is to make sure of yourself."

Leslie : "I will, mamma, I will. He must go; oh, yes, he must go! I see that it would n't do. It would be too unequal, — I 'm so far beneath him in everything but the things I ought to despise. No, I 'm not his equal, and I never can be, and so I must not think of him any more. If *he* were rich, and had been brought up like me, and I were some poor girl with nothing but her love for him, he would never let the world outweigh her love, as I do his. Don't praise me, mother; don't thank me. It is n't for you I do it; it is n't for anything worthy, or true, or good; it 's because I 'm a coward, and afraid of the opinions of people I despise. You 've shown me what I am. I thought I was brave and strong; but I am weak and timid, and I shall never respect myself any more. Send him away; tell him what an abject creature I am! It will kill me to have him think meanly of me, but oh, it will be a thousand times better that he should have a right to scorn me now, than that I should ever come to despise myself for having been ashamed of him, when — when — That I *could n't* bear!" She drops into a chair near the table and lets fall her face into her hands upon it, sobbing.

Mrs. Bellingham: "Leslie, Leslie! Be yourself! How strangely you act!"

Leslie, lifting her face, to let it gleam a moment upon her mother before she drops it: " Oh, yes, I *feel* very strangely. But now I won't distress you any more, mother," lifting her face again and impetuously drying her eyes with her handkerchief; "I will be firm, now, and no one shall ever hear a murmur from me, — not a murmur. I think that's due to you, mamma; you have been so patient with me. I've no right to grieve you by going on in this silly way, and I won't. I will be firm, firm, firm!" She casts herself into her mother's arms, and as she hangs upon her neck in a passion of grief, Mrs. Murray appears in the door-way, and in spite of Mrs. Bellingham's gesticulated entreaties to retire, advances into the room.

II.

MRS. MURRAY, MRS. BELLINGHAM, *and* LESLIE.

Mrs. Murray : " Why, what in the world does all this mean ? "

Leslie, raising her head and turning fiercely upon her: " It means that I'm now all you wish me to be, — quite your own ideal of ingratitude and selfishness, and I wish you joy of your success ! " She vanishes stormily from the room and leaves Mrs. Murray planted.

Mrs. Murray: " Has she dismissed him ? Has she broken with him ? "

Mrs. Bellingham, coldly : " I think she meant you to understand that."

Mrs. Murray: " Very well, then, Charles can't come a moment too soon. If things are at this pass, and Leslie's in this mood, it's the most dangerous moment of the whole affair. If she should meet him now, everything would be lost."

Mrs. Bellingham: "Don't be troubled. She won't meet him; he's gone."

Mrs. Murray: "I shall believe that when I see him going. A man like that would never leave her, in the world, because she bade him, — and I should think him a great fool if he did."

V.

BLAKE'S SAVING DOUBT.

LESLIE *and* MAGGIE.

Leslie: "But it's all over,—it's all over. I shall live it down; but it will make another girl of me, Maggie." Along the road that winds near the nook where the encounter with the tramps took place, Leslie comes languidly pacing with her friend Maggie Wallace, who listens, as they walk, with downcast eyes and an air of reverent devotion, to Leslie's talk. Her voice trembles a little, and as they pause a moment Maggie draws Leslie's head down upon her neck, from which the latter presently lifts it fiercely. "I don't *wish* you to pity me, Maggie, for I don't deserve any pity. I'm not suffering an atom more than I ought. It's all my own fault. Mamma really left me quite free, and if I cared more for what people would say and think and *look* than I did for him, I'm rightfully punished, and I'm not going to whimper about it.   I've thought it all out."

Maggie : " O Leslie, you always *did* think things out so clearly ! "

Leslie : "And I hope that I shall get my reward, and be an example.   I hope I shall never marry at all, or else some horrid old thing I detest ; it would serve me right and I should be glad of it ! "

Maggie : " Oh no, no !   Don't talk in that way, Leslie.   Do come back with me to the house and lie down, or I'm sure you'll be ill.   You look perfectly worn out."

Leslie, drooping upon the fallen log where she had sat to sketch the birch forest: " Yes, I'm tired. I think I shall never be rested again.   It's the same   place," — looking   wistfully   round, — " and yet how strange it seems.   You know we used to come here, and sit on this log and talk.   What long, long talks !   Oh me, it will never be again ! How weird those birches look !   Like ghosts.   I wish I was one of them.   Well, well !   It's all over.   Don't wait here, Maggie, dear.   Go back to the house ; I will come soon ; you must n't let

me keep you from Miss Roberts. Excuse me to
her, and tell her I'll go some other time. I can't,
now. Go, Maggie!"

Maggie: "O Leslie; I hate to leave you here!
After what's happened, it seems such a dreadful
place."

Leslie: "After what's happened, it's a sacred
place, — the dearest place in the world to me.
Come, Maggie, you mustn't break your appoint-
ment. It was very good of you to come with me
at all, and now you must go. Say that you left me
behind a little way ; that I'll be there directly."

Maggie: "Leslie!"

Leslie: "Maggie!" They embrace tenderly,
and Maggie, looking back more than once, goes on
her way, while Leslie sits staring absently at the
birches. She remains in this dreary reverie till she
is startled by a footfall in the road, when she rises
in a sudden panic. Blake listlessly advances toward her ; at the sight of her he halts, and they
both stand silently regarding each other.

II.

LESLIE *and* BLAKE.

Leslie : " Oh ! You said you were going away."

Blake : " Are you in such haste to have me gone? I had to wait for the afternoon stage; I could n't walk. I thought I might keep faith with you by staying away from the house till it was time to start."

Leslie, precipitately : " Do you call that keeping faith with me ? Is leaving me all alone keeping — Oh, yes, yes, it is ! You have done right. It 's I who can't keep faith with myself. Why did you come here ? You knew I would be here ! I did n't think you could be guilty of such duplicity."

Blake : " I had no idea of finding you here, but if I had known you were here perhaps I could n't have kept away. The future does n't look very bright to me, Miss Bellingham. I had a crazy

notion that perhaps I might somehow find something of the past here that I could make my own.
I wanted to come and stand here, and think once
more that it all really happened — that here I saw
the pity in your face that made me so glad of my
hurt."

Leslie: "No; stop! It was n't pity! It was
nothing good or generous. It was mean regret
that I should be under such an obligation to you;
it was a selfish and despicable fear that you would
have a claim upon my acquaintance which I must
recognize." Blake makes a gesture of protest and
disbelief, and seems about to speak, but she hurries
on: "You must n't go away with one good thought
of me. Since we parted, three hours ago, I have
learned to know myself as I never did before, and
now I see what a contemptible thing I am. I flattered myself that I had begged you to go away
because I did n't like to cross the wishes of my
family, but it was n't that. It was — oh, listen! and
try if you can imagine such vileness: I 'm so much
afraid of the world I 've always lived in, that no
matter how good and brave and wise and noble

you were, still if any one should laugh or sneer at
you because you had been — what you have been
— I should be ashamed of you. There! I'm so
low and feeble a creature as that; and that's the
real reason why you must go and forget me; and I
must not think and you must not think it's from
any good motive I send you away."

Blake: " I don't believe it! "

Leslie: " What! "

Blake: " I don't believe what you say. Nothing
shall rob me of my faith in you. Do you think
that I'm not man enough to give up what I've no
right to because it's the treasure of the world?
Do you think I can't go till you make me believe
that what I'd have sold my life for is n't worth a
straw? No! I'll give up my hope, I'll give up
my love, — poor fool I was to let it live an instant! — but my faith in you is something dearer
yet, and I'll keep that till I die. Say what you
will, you are still first among women to me: the
most beautiful, the noblest, the best! "

Leslie, gasping, and arresting him in a movement
to turn away: " Wait, wait; don't go! Speak;

say it again! Say that you don't believe it; that
it is n't true!'"

Blake: "No, I don't believe it. No, it is n't
true. It's abominably false!"

Leslie, bursting into tears: "Oh yes, it is. It's
abominable, and it's false. Yes, I *will* believe in
myself again. I *know* that if I had cared for—
any one, as—as you cared, as you said you cared
for me, I could be as true to them as you would be
through any fate. Oh, thank you, thank you!"
At the tearful joy of the look she turns on him he
starts toward her. "Oh!"—she shrinks away—
"you must n't think that I"—

Blake: "I don't think anything that does n't
worship you!"

Leslie: "Yes, but what I said sounds just like
the other, when you misunderstood me so heart-
lessly."

Blake: "I don't misunderstand you now. You
do tell me that you love me, don't you? How
should I dare hope without your leave?"

Leslie: "You said you would n't have taken me
as a gift if I had. You said you'd have hated me.
You said"—

Blake: "I was all wrong in what I thought. I'm ashamed to think of that; but I was right in what I said."

Leslie: "Oh, *were* you! If you could misunderstand me then, how do you know that you're not misunderstanding me now?"

Blake : "Perhaps I am. Perhaps I'm dreaming as wildly as I was then. But you shall say. Am I?"

Leslie, demurely : "I don't know; I" — staying his instantaneous further approach with extended arm — "No, no!" She glances fearfully round "Wait; come with me. Come back with me — that is, if you will."

Blake, passionately : "If I will!"

Leslie, with pensive archness: "I want you to help me clear up my character."

Blake, gravely : " Leslie, may I" —

Leslie : "I can't talk with you here."

Blake, sadly: "I will not go back with you to make sorrow for you and trouble among your friends. It's enough to know that you don't forbid me to love you."

Leslie : " Oh no, it is n't enough — for every-body."

Blake : " Leslie " —

Leslie : " Miss Bellingham, please ! "

Blake : " Miss Bellingham " —

Leslie : " Well ? "

Blake, after a stare of rapturous perplexity : " Nothing ! "

Leslie, laughing through her tears : " If you don't make haste you will be too late for the stage, and then you can't get away till to-morrow."

VI.

MR. CHARLES BELLINGHAM'S DIPLOMACY.

I.

Mrs. Bellingham, Mrs. Murray, *and* Mr. Charles Bellingham.

In the parlor with Mrs. Bellingham and Mrs. Murray sits a gentleman no longer young, but in the bloom of a comfortable middle life, with blonde hair tending to baldness, accurately parted in the middle, and with a handsome face, lazily shrewd, supported by a comely substructure of double chin, and traversed by a full blonde mustache. He is simply, almost carelessly, yet elegantly dressed in a thin summer stuff, and he has an effect of recent arrival. His manner has distinction, enhanced and refined by the eye-glasses which his near-sightedness obliges him to wear. He sits somewhat ponderously in the chair in which he has planted a person just losing its earlier squareness in the lines of beauty; his feet are set rather wide apart in the fashion of gentlemen approaching a certain weight;

and he has an air of amiable resolution as of a man who having dined well yesterday means to dine well to-day.

Charles Bellingham, smiling amusement and indolently getting the range of his aunt through his glasses: "So I have come a day after the fair."

Mrs. Murray: "That is your mother's opinion."

Mrs. Bellingham: "Yes, Charles, Leslie had known what to do herself, and had done it, even before I spoke to her. I'm sorry we made you drag all the way up here, for nothing."

Bellingham: "Oh, I don't mind it, mother. Duty called, and I obeyed. My leisure can wait for my return. The only thing is that they've got a new fellow at the club now, who interprets one's ideas of planked Spanish mackerel with a sentiment that amounts to genius. I suppose you plank horn-pout, here. But as to coming for nothing, I'd much rather do that than come for something, in a case like this. You say Leslie saw herself that it would n't do?"

Mrs. Bellingham: "Yes, she had really behaved admirably, Charles; and when I set the whole matter before her, she fully agreed with me."

Bellingham : " But you think she rather liked him ? "

Mrs. Bellingham, sighing a little : " Yes, there is no doubt of that."

Bellingham, musingly : " Well, it's a pity. Behaved rather well in that tramp business, you said ? "

Mrs. Bellingham : " Nobly."

Bellingham : " And has n't pushed himself, at all ? "

Mrs. Bellingham : "Not an instant."

Bellingham : " Well, I'm sorry for him, poor fellow, but I'm glad the thing's over. It would have been an awkward affair, under all the circumstances, to take hold of. I say, mother," — with a significant glance at Mrs. Murray, — " there has n't been anything — ah — abrupt in the management of this matter ? You ladies sometimes forget the limitations of action in your amiable eagerness to have things over, you know."

Mrs. Bellingham : " I think your mother would not forget herself in such a case."

Bellingham : " Of course, of course ; excuse my

asking, mother. But you're about the only
woman that would n't."

Mrs. Murray, bitterly : " Oh, your mother and
Leslie have *both* used him with the greatest tender-
ness."

Bellingham, dryly : " I 'm glad to hear it ; I
never doubted it. If the man had been treated
by any of my family with the faintest slight after
what had happened, I should have felt bound as
a gentleman to offer him any reparation in my
power, — to make him any apology. People of
our sort can't do anything shabby." Mrs. Murray
does not reply, but rises from her place on the sofa
and goes to the window. " Does Leslie know I 'm
here ? "

Mrs. Bellingham, with a little start : " Really, I
forgot to tell her you were coming to-day ; we had
been keeping it from her, and " —

Bellingham : " I don't know that it matters.
Where is she ? "

Mrs. Bellingham : " I saw her going out with
Maggie Wallace. I dare say she will be back
soon."

Bellingham: "All right. Where is the young man? Has he gone yet?"

Mrs. Bellingham: "No, he could n't go till the afternoon stage leaves. He 's still here."

Bellingham: "I must look him up, and make my acknowledgments to him." He rises. "By the way, what 's his name?"

Mrs. Murray, standing with her face toward the window, leans forward and inclines to this side and that, as if to make perfectly sure before speaking of some fact of vivid interest which seems to have caught her notice, and at the moment Bellingham puts his question summons her sister-in-law in a voice of terrible incrimination and triumph: "Marion, did you say Leslie had gone out with Maggie Wallace?"

Mrs. Bellingham, indifferently: "Yes."

Mrs. Murray: "Will you be kind enough to step here?" Mrs. Bellingham, with a little lady-like surprise, approaches, and Mrs. Murray indicates with a stabbing thrust of her hand, the sight which has so much interested her: "Does *that* look as if it were all over?"

Bellingham, carelessly, as Mrs. Bellingham with great evident distress remains looking in the direction indicated: " What 's the matter now?"

Mrs. Murray: " Nothing. I merely wished your mother to enjoy a fresh proof of Leslie's discretion. She is returning to tell us that it 's out of the question in company with the young man himself."

Bellingham: " Wha — ha, ha, ha! — *What?* "

Mrs. Murray: " She is returning with the young man from whom she had just parted forever."

Bellingham, approaching: " Oh, come now, aunt."

Mrs. Murray, fiercely: " Will you look for yourself, if you don't believe me? "

Bellingham: " Oh, I believe you, fast enough, but as for looking, you know I could n't tell the man in the moon at this distance, if Leslie happened to be walking home with him. But is the — ah — fat necessarily in the fire, because " — Mrs. Murray whirls away from Bellingham where he remains with his hands on his hips peering over his mother's shoulder, and pounces upon a large opera-glass which stands on the centre-table, and returning with it thrusts it at him. "Eh? What?"

Mrs. Murray, excitedly: "It's what we watch the loons on the lake with."

Bellingham: "Well, but I don't see the application. They're not loons on the lake."

Mrs. Murray: "No; but they're loons on the land, and it comes to the same thing." She vehemently presses the glass upon him.

Bellingham, gravely: "Do you mean, aunt, that you actually want me to watch my sister through an opera-glass, like a shabby Frenchman at a watering-place? Thanks. I could never look Les in the face again. It's a little too much like eavesdropping." He folds his arms, and regards his aunt with reproachful amazement, while she dashes back to set the glass on the table again.

Mrs. Bellingham, in great trouble: "Wait, Kate. Charles, dear, I — I think you must."

Bellingham: "What?"

Mrs. Bellingham: "Yes, you had better look. You will have to proceed in this matter now, and you must form some conclusions beforehand."

Bellingham: "But mother" —

Mrs. Bellingham, anxiously : " Don't worry me, Charles.   I think you must."

Bellingham : " All right, mother."   He unfolds his arms and accepts the glass from her.   " I never knew you to take an unfair advantage, and I 'll obey you on trust.   But I tell you I don't like it. I don't like it at all," — getting the focus, with several trials; " I 've never stolen sheep, but I think I can realize, now, something of the self-reproach which misappropriated mutton might bring.   *Where* did you say they were?   Oh, over there!   *I* was looking off here, at that point.   They 're coming this way, are n't they ? "   With a start : " Hollo ! She 's got his arm !   Oh, *that* won't do.   I 'm surprised at Les doing that, unless " — continuing to look —   " By Jove !   He 's not a bad-looking fellow, at all.   He —   Why, confound it !   No, it can't be !   Why, yes — no — yes, it is, it *is* — by Heaven, it *is* — by all that 's strange it is — BLAKE ! "   He lets the glass fall ; and stands glaring at his aunt and mother, who confront him in speechless mystification.   ·

Mrs. Bellingham : " Blake?   Why, of course it 's Blake.   We *told* you it was Mr. Blake ! "

Bellingham: "No, I beg your pardon, mother, you did n't! You never told me it was anybody — by name."

Mrs. Bellingham: "Well?"

Bellingham: "Why, don't you understand, mother? It's *my* Blake!"

Mrs. Bellingham: "*Your* Blake? *Your* — Charles, what *do* you mean?"

Bellingham: "Why, I mean that this is the man" — giving his glasses a fresh pinch on his nose with his thumb and forefinger — "that fished me out of the Mississippi. I flatter myself he could n't do it now. 'The grossness of my nature would have weight to drag him down,' — *both* of us down. But he'd try it, and he'd have the pluck to go down with me if he failed. Come, mother, you see *I* can't do anything in this matter. It's simply impossible. It's out of the question."

Mrs. Murray: "*Why* is it out of the question?"

Bellingham: "Well, I don't know that I can explain, aunt Kate, if it is n't clear to you, already."

Mrs. Bellingham, recovering from the dismay in which her son's words have plunged her:

"Charles, Charles! Do you mean that this Mr Blake is the person who saved you from "—

Bellingham: "From a watery grave? I do, mother."

Mrs. Bellingham: "There *must* be some mistake. You can't tell at this distance, Charles."

Bellingham: "There's no mistake, mother. I should know Blake on the top of Ponkwasset. He was rather more than a casual acquaintance, you see. By Jove, I can't think of the matter with any sort of repose. I can see it all now, just as if it were somebody else: I was weighted down down with my accoutrements, and I went over the side of the boat like a flash, and under that yellow deluge like a bullet. I had just leisure to think what a shame it was my life should go for nothing at a time when we needed men so much, when I felt a grip on my hair," — rubbing his bald spot, — "it could n't be done now! Then I knew I was all right, and waited for developments. The only development was Blake. He fought shy of me, if you'll believe it, after that, till I closed with him one day and had it out with him, and convinced

him that he had done rather a handsome thing by
me. But that was the end of it. I could n't get
him to stand anything else in the way of gratitude.
Blake had a vice : he was proud."

Mrs. Bellingham : " And what became of him ? "

Bellingham : " Who ? Blake ? He was the
engineer of the boat, I ought to explain. He was
transferred to a gunboat after that, and I believe
he stuck to it throughout the fighting on the Mississippi. It 's — let me see — it 's five years now
since I saw him in Nebraska, when I went out
there to grow up with the country, and found I
could n't wait for it." After a pause : " I don't
know what it was about Blake ; but he somehow
made everybody feel that there was stuff in him.
In the three weeks we were together we became
great friends, and I must say I never liked a man
better. Well, that 's why, aunt Kate."

Mrs. Murray : " I don't see that it has anything
whatever to do with the matter. The question is
whether you wish Leslie to marry a man of his
station and breeding, or not. His goodness and
greatness have nothing to do with it. The fact re-

mains that he is not at all her equal — that he
is n't a gentleman " —

Bellingham: "Oh, come now, aunt Kate.
You 're not going to tell me that a man who saved
my life is n't a gentleman ? "

Mrs. Murray: "And you 're not going to tell
me that a steamboat engineer is a gentleman ? "

Bellingham, disconcerted: " Eh ? "

Mrs. Murray: "The question is, are you going
to abandon that unhappy girl to her fancy for a
man totally unfit to be her husband simply because
he happened to save your life ? "

Bellingham: " Why, you see, aunt Kate" —

Mrs. Murray: "Do you think it would be gentlemanly to do it ? "

Bellingham: " Well, if you put it that way, no,
I don't. And if you want to know, I don't see
my way to behaving like a gentleman in this con-
nection, whatever I do." He scratches his head
ruefully: "The fact is that the advantages are all
on Blake's side, and he 'll have to manage very
badly if he does n't come out the only gentleman
in the business." After a moment: " How was it

you did n't put the name and the — a — profession together, mother, and reflect that this *was* my Blake ? "

Mrs. Bellingham, with plaintive reproach : " Charles, you know how uncommunicative you were about all your life as a soldier. You never told me half so much about this affair before, and you never — it seems very heartless now that I did n't insist on knowing, but at the time it was only part of the nightmare in which we were living — you never told me his name before."

Bellingham : " Did n't I ? Well ! I supposed I had, of course. Um ! That was too bad. I say, mother, Blake has never let anything drop that made you think he had ever known me, or done me any little favor, I suppose ? "

Mrs. Bellingham : " No, not the slightest hint. If he had only " —

Bellingham : " Ah, that was like him, confound him ! " Bellingham muses again with a hopeless air, and then starts suddenly from his reverie : " Why, the fact is, you know, mother, Blake is really a magnificent fellow ; and you know — well, I *like* him ! "

Mrs. Murray : "Oh! That's Leslie's excuse ! "

Bellingham : "Eh ? "

Mrs. Murray : "If you are going to take Leslie's part, it's fortunate you have common ground. *Like* him ! "

Bellingham : "Mother, what is the unhallowed hour for dinner in these wilds ? One o'clock ? I've a fancy for tackling this business after dinner."

Mrs. Bellingham : "I'm afraid, my dear, that it can't be put off. They must be here, soon."

Bellingham, sighing : "Well ! Though they didn't seem to be hurrying."

Mrs. Murray, bitterly: "If they could only know what a friendly disposition there was towards him here, I'm sure they'd make haste ! "

Bellingham : "Um ! "

Mrs. Bellingham, after a pause : "You don't know anything about his — his — family, do you, Charles ? "

Bellingham : "No, mother, I don't. My impression is that he *has* no family, any more than

— Adam ; or — protoplasm. All I know about him is that he was from first to last one of those natural gentlemen that upset all your preconceived notions of those things. His associations must have been commoner than — well it's impossible to compare them to anything satisfactory ; but I never saw a trait in him or heard a word from him that was n't refined. He gave me the impression of a very able man, too, as I was just saying, but where his strength lay, I can't say."

Mrs. Bellingham : " Leslie says he's an inventor."

Bellingham: " Well, very likely. I remember, now : he was a machinist by trade, I believe, and he was an enlisted man on the boat when the engineer was killed ; and Blake was the man who could step right into his place. It was considered a good thing amongst those people. He was a reader in his way, and most of the time he had some particularly hard-headed book in his hand when he was off duty, — about physics or metaphysics ; used to talk them up now and then, very well. I never had any doubt about his coming

out all right. He's a baffler, Blake is, — at least
he is, for me. Now I suppose aunt Kate, here,
does n't find him baffling, at all. She takes our little standards, our little weights and measures, and
tests him with them, and she's perfectly satisfied
with the result. It's a clear case of won't do."

Mrs. Murray: "Do you say it is n't?"

Bellingham: "No; I merely doubt if it is.
You don't doubt, and there you have the advantage
of me. You always were a selected oyster, aunt
Kate, and you always knew that you could n't be
improved upon. Now, I'm a selected oyster, too,
apparently, but I'm not certain that I'm the best
choice that could have been made. I'm a *huitre
de mon siècle;* I am the ill-starred mollusk that
doubts. Of course we can't go counter to the
theory that God once created people and no-people,
and that they have nothing to do but to go on re-
producing themselves and leave him at leisure for
the rest of eternity. But really, aunt Kate, I have
seen some things in my time — and I don't mind
saying Blake is one of them — that made me think
the Creator was still — active. I admit that it

sounds " — fitting his glasses on — "rather absurd for an old diner-out like myself to say it."

Mrs. Murray, with energy : "All this is neither here nor there, Charles, and you know it. The simple question is whether you wish your sister to marry a man whose past you 'll be ashamed to be frank about. I 'll admit, if you like, that he 's quite our equal, — our superior ; but what are you going to do with your ex-steamboat engineer in society ? "

Bellingham, dubiously : "Well, it would be rather awkward."

Mrs. Murray : "How will you introduce him, and what will you say to people about his family and his station and business ? Or do you mean to banish yourself and give up the world which you find so comfortable for the boon of a brother-in-law whom you don't really know from Adam ? "

Bellingham : "Well, I must allow the force of your argument. "Yes," — after a gloomy little reverie, — "you 're right. It won't do. It *is* out of the question. I 'll put an end to it, — if it does n't put an end to me. That ' weird seizure ' as of misappropriated mutton oppresses me again. Mother, I think you'd better go away, — you and aunt Kate, — and let me meet him and Leslie here alone, when they come in. Or, I say: if you could detach Les, and let him come in here by himself, somehow? I don't suppose it can be done. Nothing seems disposed to let itself be done."

Mrs. Bellingham: "Charles, I'm sorry this disagreeable business should fall to you."

Bellingham: "Oh, don't mind it, mother. What's a brother for, if he can't be called upon to break off his sister's love affairs? But I don't deny it's a nasty business."

Mrs. Murray, in retiring : "I sincerely hope he'll make it so for you, and cure you of your absurdities."

BELLINGHAM *and* MRS. BELLINGHAM; LESLIE *and* BLAKE, *without.*

Bellingham: "O Parthian shaft! Wish me well out of it, mother!"

Mrs. Bellingham, sighing: "I do, Charles; I do with all my heart. You have the most difficult duty that a gentleman ever had to perform. I don't see how you're to take hold of it; I don't, indeed."

Bellingham: "Well, it *is* embarrassing. But it's a noble cause, and I suppose Heaven will befriend me. The trouble is, don't you know, I have n't got any — any point of view, any tenable point of view. It won't do to act simply in our own interest; *we* can't do *that*, mother; we're not the sort. I must try to do it in Blake's behalf, and that's what I don't see my way to, exactly. What I wish to do is to make my interference a magnanimous benefaction to Blake, — something that he 'll recognize in after years with gratitude as a — a mysterious Providence. If I 've got to be a snob, mother, I wish to be a snob on the highest possible grounds."

Mrs. Bellingham: "Don't use that word, Charles. It 's shocking."

Bellingham: "Well, I won't, mother. I say: can't you think of some disqualifications in Leslie, that I could make a *point d'appui* in a conscientious effort to serve Blake?"

Mrs. Bellingham: "Charles!"

Bellingham: "I mean, is n't she rather a worldly, frivolous, fashionable spirit, devoted to pleasure, and incapable of sympathizing with — with his higher moods, don't you know? Something like that?" Bellingham puts his thumbs in his waistcoat pockets and inclines towards his mother with a hopeful smile.

Mrs. Bellingham: "No, Charles; you know she is nothing of the kind. She 's a girl and she likes amusement, but I should like to see the man whose moods were too lofty for Leslie. She is everything that 's generous and true and high-minded."

Bellingham, scratching his head: "That's bad! Then she is n't — ah — she has n't any habits of extravagance that would unfit her to be the wife of a poor man who — ah — had his way to make in the world?"

Mrs. Bellingham: "She never spends half her allowance on herself; and besides, Charles, (how ridiculously you talk!) she has all that money your uncle left her, and if she marries him, he won't be poor any longer."

Bellingham, eagerly: "And that would ruin his career! Still " — after a moment's thought — "I don't see how I'm to use that idea, exactly. No, I shall have to fall back on the good old ground that it's simply — out of the question. I think that's good ; it has a thorough, logical, and final sound. I shall stick to that. Well, leave me to my fate! — Hollo! That's Blake's voice, now. I don't wonder it takes Leslie. It's the most sympathetic voice in the world. They're coming up here, are n't they? You'd better go, mother. I wish you could have got Leslie away " —

Leslie, without: "Wait for me, there. I must

go to mamma's room at once, and tell her everything."

Blake, without : " Of course.   And say that I
wish to see her."

Leslie : " Good-by."

Blake : " Good-by."

Leslie : " We won't keep you long.   *Good-*by."

Blake : " *Good-*by."   As he enters one of the
parlor doors, flushed and radiant, Mrs. Bellingham
retreats through the other.

III.

BLAKE *and* BELLINGHAM.

Bellingham, coming promptly forward to greet Blake, with both hands extended: "Blake!"

Blake, after a moment of stupefaction: "Bellingham!"

Bellingham: "My dear old fellow!" He wrings Blake fervently by the left hand. "This is the most astonishing thing in the world! To find you here — in New England — with my people; it's the most wonderful thing that ever was! They 've been — ah — been telling me all about you, my mother has; and I want to thank you — you look uncommonly well, Blake, and not a day older! Do you mean to go through life with that figure? — thank you for all you 've done for them; and — I don't know: what does a man say to a fellow who has behaved as you did in that business with the tramps?"— wringing Blake's left hand again and gently touching his right arm in its sling. "By Jove, old fellow! I don't know what to say, to *you*; I — Do you think it was quite the thing, though, not to intimate that you'd known *me*? Come, now; that wasn't fair. It wasn't frank. It wasn't like *you*, Blake. Hey?" He affectionately presses Blake's hand at every emphatic word.

Blake, releasing himself: "I didn't like it: but I couldn't help it. It would have seemed to claim something, and I should have had to allow — they would have found out "—

Bellingham: "That you happened to save my life, once. Well, upon my word, I don't think it was a thing to be ashamed of; at least, at that time; I was in the army, then. At present — I don't know that I should blame you for hushing the matter up."

Blake, who has turned uneasily away, and has apparently not been paying the closest attention to Bellingham's reproaches, but now confronts him: "I suppose you're a gentleman, Bellingham."

Bellingham, taking the abruptness of Blake's question with amiable irony : " There have been moments in which I have flattered myself to that degree ; even existence itself is problematical, to my mind, at other times : but — well, yes, I suppose I am a gentleman. The term's conventional. And then ? "

Blake : " I mean that you 're a fair-minded, honest man, and that I can talk to you without the risk of being misunderstood or having any sort of meanness attributed to me ? "

Bellingham : " I should have to be a much shabbier fellow than I am, for anything of that sort, Blake."

Blake : " I did n't expect to find you here ; I was expecting to speak with your mother. But I don't see why I should n't say to you what I have to say. In fact, I think I can say it better to you."

Bellingham : " Thanks, Blake ; you 'll always find me your — That is — well, go ahead ! "

Blake : " You don't think I 'm a man to do anything sneaking, do you ? "

Bellingham: "Again? My dear fellow, that goes without saying. It's out of the question."

Blake, walking up and down, and stopping from time to time while he speaks in a tone of passionate self-restraint: "Well, I'm glad to hear that, because I know that to some the thing might have a different look." After a pause, in which Blake takes another turn round the room and arrives in front of Bellingham again: "If your people have been telling you about me, I suppose they've hinted — but I don't care to know it — that they think I'm in love with Miss Bellingham, your sister. I am!" He looks at Bellingham, who remains impassive behind the glitter of his eye-glasses: "Do you see any reason why I should n't be?"

Bellingham, reluctantly: "N-no."

Blake: "I believe — no, I *can't* believe it! — but I *know* that Miss Bellingham permits it; that she — I can't say it! Is there any — any reason why I should n't ask her mother's leave to ask her to be my wife? Why, of course, there is! — a thousand, million reasons in my unworthiness; I know that. But is there" —

Bellingham, abruptly : "Blake, my dear fellow — my dear, good old boy — it won't do; it's out of the question ! It is, it is indeed ! It won't do at all. Confound it, man ! You know I like you, that I've always wanted to be a great deal more your friend than you would ever let me. Don't ask me why, but take my word for it when I tell you it's out of the question. There are a thousand reasons, as you say, though there is n't one of them in any fault of yours, old fellow. But I can't give them. It won't do !" Bellingham in his turn begins to walk up and down the room with a face of acute misery and hopelessness, and at the last word he stops and stares helplessly into Blake's eyes, who has remained in his place.

Blake, with suppressed feeling : "Do you expect me to be satisfied with that answer ? "

Bellingham, at first confused and then with a burst of candor : " No ; I would n't, myself." His head falls, and a groan breaks from his lips : " This is the roughest thing I ever knew of. Hang it, Blake, don't you see what a — a — box I'm in ? People pulling and hauling at me, and hammering away on all sides, till I don't know which end I'm standing on! You would n't like it yourself. Why do you ask? Why must you be — ah — satisfied? Come! Why don't you let it all — go?"

Blake: "Upon my word, Bellingham, you talk" —

Bellingham: "Like a fool! I know it. And it's strictly in character. At the present moment I *feel* like a fool. I *am* a fool! By Jove, if I ever supposed I should get into such a tight place as this! Why, don't you see, Blake, what an extremely unfair advantage you have of me? Deuce take it, man, *I* have some rights in the matter, too, I fancy!"

Blake, bewildered: "Rights? Advantage? I don't understand all this."

Bellingham: "How not understand?"

Blake, gazing in mystified silence at Bellingham for a brief space, and then resuming more steadily: "There's some objection to me, that's clear enough. I don't make any claim, but you would think I ought to know what the matter is, would n't you?"

Bellingham : " Y-yes, Blake."

Blake : " I know that I'm ten years older than Miss Bellingham, and that it might look as if " —

Bellingham, hastily : " Oh, not in the least — not in the least ! "

Blake: " Our acquaintance was n't regularly made, I believe. But you don't suppose that I urged it, or that it would have been kept up if it had n't been for their kindness and for chances that nobody foresaw ? "

Bellingham : " There is n't a circumstance of the whole affair that is n't perfectly honorable to you, Blake ; that is n't *like* you. Confound it " —

Blake : " I won't ask you whether you think I thought of her being rich ? "

Bellingham : " No, sir ! That would be offensive."

Blake : " Then what is it ? Is there some personal objection to me with your family ? "

Bellingham: " There is n't at all, Blake, I assure you."

Blake : " Then I don't understand, and " — with rising spirit — " I want to say once for all that I

11

think your leaving me to ask these things and put myself on the defensive in this way, begging you for this reason and for that, is n't what I 'm used to. But I 'm like a man on trial for his life, and I stand it. Now, go on and say what there is to say. Don't spare my feelings, man! I have no pride where *she* is concerned. What do you know against me that makes it impossible?"

Bellingham: "O Lord! It is n't *against* you. It 's nothing personal; personally we 've all reason to respect and honor you; you 've done us nothing but good in the handsomest way. But it won't do for all that. There 's an incompatibility —a—a—*I* don't know what to call it! Confound it, Blake! You know very well that there 's none of that cursed nonsense about me. *I* don't care what a man is in life; I only ask what he is in himself. I accept the American plan in good faith. I know all sorts of fellows; devilish good fellows some of them are, too! Why, I had that Mitchell, who behaved so well at the Squattick Mills disaster, to dine with me; went down and looked him up, and had him to dine with me.

Some of the men did n't think it was the thing; but I can assure you that he talked magnificently about the affair. I drew him out, and before we were done we had the whole room about us. I would n't have missed it on any account. That 's *my* way."

Blake, dryly: " It 's a very magnanimous way. The man must have felt honored."

Bellingham: " What ? — Oh, deuce take it ! *I* don't mean any of that patronizing rot, you know I don't. You know I think such a man as that ten times as good as myself. What I mean is that it 's different with women. They have n't got the same — what shall I say ? — horizons, social horizons, don't you know. *They* can't accept a man for what he is in himself. They have to take him for what he *is n't* in himself. They have to have their world carried on upon the European plan, in short. I don't know whether I make myself understood " —

Blake, with hardness: " Yes, you do. The objection is to my having been " —

Bellingham, hastily interposing : " Well — ah —

no ! I can't admit that. It is n't the occupation.
We've all been occupied more or less remotely in
—in some sort of thing ; a man's a fool who tries
to blink that. But I don't know that I can make
it clear how our belonging, now, to a different
order of things makes our women distrustful — I
won't say skeptical, but anxious — as to the in-
fluence of — ah — other social circumstances.
They're mere creatures of tradition, women are,
and where you or I, Blake," — with caressing good
comradeship and the assumption of an impartial
high-mindedness, — "would n't care a straw for a
man's trade or profession, *they* are more disposed
to — ah — particularize, and — don't you know —
distinguish ! "

Blake, gravely : "I tried to make Miss Bellingham understand from the first just what I was and
had been. I certainly never concealed anything.
Do you think she would care for what disturbs the
other ladies of your family ? "

Bellingham : "Leslie ? Well, she's still a very
young girl, and she has streaks of originality that
rather disqualify her for appreciating — ah —

She's romantic! I'm sure I'm greatly obliged to you, Blake, for taking the thing in this reasonable way. You know how to sympathize with one's extreme reluctance — and — ah — embarrassment in putting a case of the kind."

Blake, with a sad, musing tone: "Yes, God knows I'm sorry for you. I don't suppose you like to do it."

Bellingham: "Thanks, thanks, Blake. It was quite as much on your own account that I spoke. They would make it deucedly uncomfortable for you in the family, — there's no end to the aunts and grandmothers, and things, and you'd make them uncomfortable too, with your — history." Mopping his forehead with his handkerchief: "You have it infernally hot, up here, don't you?"

Blake, still musingly: "Then you think that Miss Bellingham herself would n't be seriously distressed?"

Bellingham: "Leslie's a girl that will go through anything she's made up her mind to. And if she likes you well enough to marry you" —

Blake: "She says so."

Bellingham : " Then burning plowshares would n't
have the smallest effect upon her.   But " —

Blake, quietly : " Then I won't give her up."

Bellingham : " Eh ? "

Blake : " I won't give her up.   It 's bad enough
as it is, but if I were such a sneak as to leave the
woman who loved me because my marrying her
would be awkward for her friends, I should be ten
thousand times unworthier than I am.   I am going
to hold to my one chance of showing myself worthy to win her, and if she will have me I will have
her, though it smashes the whole social structure.
Bellingham, you 're mistaken about this thing ;
her happiness won't depend upon the success of
the aunts and cousins in accounting for me to the
world ; it 'll depend upon whether I 'm man
enough to be all the world to her.   If she thinks
I am, I *will* be ! "

Bellingham : " Oh, don't talk in that illogical
way, Blake.   Confound it !   I know ; I can account for your state of feeling, and all that ; but I
do assure you it 's mistaken.   Let me put it to you.
You don't see this matter as I do ; you can't.
The best part of a woman's life is social " —

Blake: "I don't believe that."

Bellingham: "Well, no matter: it's so; and whether you came into Leslie's world or took her out of it, you'd make no end of — of — row. She'd suffer in a thousand ways."

Blake: "Not if she loved me, and was the kind of girl I take her to be."

Bellingham: "Oh, yes, she would, my dear fellow; Leslie's a devilish proud girl; she'd suffer in secret, but it would try her pride in ways you don't know of. Why, only consider: she's taken by surprise in this affair; she's had no time to think " —

Blake: "She shall have my whole lifetime to make up her mind in; she shall test me in every way she will, and she may fling me away at any moment she will, and I will be her slave forever. She may give me up, but I will not give her up."

Bellingham: "Well, well! We won't dispute about terms, but I'll put it to you, yourself, Blake, — yourself. I want you to see that I'm acting for your good; that I'm your friend."

Blake: "You're her brother, and you're my

friend, whatever you say. I 've borne to have you insinuate that I 'm your inferior. Go on!" Blake's voice trembles.

Bellingham: " Oh, now! Don't take that tone! It is n't fair. It makes me feel like — like the very devil. It does, indeed. I don't mean anything of the kind. I mean simply that — that — ah — remote circumstances over which you had — ah — no control have placed you at a disadvantage, — social disadvantage. That 's all. It is n't a question of inferiority or superiority. And I merely put it to you — as a friend, mind — whether the happiness of — ah — all concerned could n't be more promptly — ah — secured by your refusing to submit to tests that might — Come now my dear fellow! She 's flattered — any woman might be — by your liking her; but when she went back to her own associations " —

Blake: "If she sees any man she likes better than me, I won't claim her. But I can't judge her by a loyalty less than my own. She will never change." Bellingham essays an answer, but after some preliminary ahs and ums, abruptly desists, and guards an evidently troubled silence, which Blake assails with jealous quickness: "What do you mean? Out with it, man!"

Bellingham: "Don't take it in that way! My dear fellow" —

Blake: "If I'm her caprice and not her choice, I want to know it! I won't be killed by inches. Speak!"

Bellingham: "Stop! I owe you my life, but you must n't take that tone with me."

Blake: "You owe me nothing, — nothing but an answer. If you mean there has been some one before me — *She* has told me that she never cared for any one but me; I believe her, but I want to know what you mean."

Bellingham: "She's my sister! What do *you* mean?"

IV.

LESLIE, BLAKE, *and* BELLINGHAM.

Leslie: "Oh, what *does* it mean?" She enters the room, as if she had been suddenly summoned by the sound of their angry voices from a guiltless ambush in the hall. At the sight of their flushed faces and defiant attitudes she flutters, electrically attracted, first toward one and then toward the other, but at last she instinctively takes shelter at Blake's elbow: " Charles, what are you saying? What are you both so angry for? Oh, I hoped to find you such good friends, and here you are quarreling! Charles, what have you been doing? O Charles, I always thought you were so generous and magnanimous, and have *you* been joining that odious conspiracy against *us?* For shame! And what have you found to say, I should like to know? I should *like* to know what you 've found to say — what a *gentleman*

COULD say, under the circumstances !" She grows more vehement as their mutual embarrassment increases upon the men, and Bellingham fades into a blank dismay behind the glitter of his eyeglasses. "Have you been saying something you're ashamed of, Charles? You *couldn't* say anything about *him*, and so you've been trying to set him against *me*. *What* have you said about your sister, Charles? — and always pretending to be so fond of me! Oh, oh, oh!" Miss Bellingham snatches her handkerchief from her pocket and hides her grief in it, while her brother remains in entire petrifaction at her prescience.

Bellingham, finally: "Why, Leslie— Deuce take it all, Blake, why don't *you* say something? I tell you, I haven't *said* anything against you, Les. Blake will tell you himself that I was merely endeavoring to set the thing before him from different points of view. I wanted him to consider the shortness of your acquaintance" —

Leslie, in her handkerchief: "It's fully three weeks since we met, — you *know* it is."

Bellingham : "And I wanted him to reflect upon

how very different all your associations and —
traditions — were " —

Leslie, still in her handkerchief: " Oh, *that* was
delicate — very ! "

Bellingham: " And to — ah — take into consideration the fact that returning to another — atmosphere — surroundings, you might — ah — change."

Leslie, lifting her face : " You did ! Charles,
did I *ever* change ? "

Bellingham : " Well, I don't know. I don't
know whether you 'd call it *changing,* exactly ; but
I certainly got the impression from aunt Kate
that there was some hope on Dudley's part last
summer " —

Leslie, quitting her refuge and advancing fiercely
upon the dismayed but immovable Bellingham
with her right hand thrust rigidly down at her side,
and her left held behind her clutching her handkerchief: " Charles, have you *dared* to intimate that I
ever cared the least thing about that — that — horrid — little — reptile ? When you *knew* that my
life was made perfectly ghastly by the way aunt
Kate forced him on me, and it was as much as I

could ever do to treat him decently! I never encouraged him for an *instant*, and you know it. Oh, Charley, Charley, how could you? It isn't for myself I care ; it's for you, for you 're a *gentleman*, and you let yourself do that! How painfully strange that low, mean, shabby feeling must have been to you! I don't wonder you could n't face me or speak to me. I don't " —

Bellingham, desperately : " Here; hold on! Good Lord! I can't stand this! Confound it, I'm not made of granite — or gutta-percha. I'll allow it was sneaking, — Blake will tell you I looked it, — but it was a desperate case. It was a family job, and I had to do my best — or my worst — as the head of the family ; and Blake would n't hear reason, and " —

Leslie : " And so you thought you 'd try *fraud !* "

Bellingham : " Well, I should n't use that word. But it 's the privilege of your sex to call a spade a pitchfork, if you don't like the spade. I tell you I never professed to know anything personally about the Dudley business and I did n't *say* anything about it; when Blake caught me up so, I was em-

barrassed to think how I might have mentioned it
in —in the heat of argument.   Come, Blake" —

Leslie, turning and going devoutly up to Blake :
" Yes, *he* will defend you. *He* must save your
honor since he saved your life."

Bellingham, with a start : " Eh ? "

Leslie : " Oh, I know about it ! Mamma told
me. She thinks just as I do, now, and she has
been feeling dreadfully about this shabby work
she 'd set you at ; but I comforted her. I told her
you would never do it in the world ; that you
would just shuffle about in your way " —

Bellingham : " Oh, thanks ! "

Leslie : " But that you had too good a heart, too
high a spirit, to breathe a syllable that would
wound the pride of a brave and generous man to
whom you owed life itself : that you would rather
die than do it ! " To Blake : " Oh, I 've always
been a romantic girl, — you won't mind it in me,
will you ? — and I 've had my foolish dreams a
thousand times about the man who risked his life
to save my brother's ; and I hoped and longed
that some day we should meet. I promised my-

self that I should know him, and I always thought how sweet and dear a privilege it would be to thank him. I want to thank you for his life as I used to dream of doing, but I cannot yet. I cannot till you tell me that he has not said one word unworthy of you, — unworthy of a gentleman ! "

Blake, smiling : " He 's all right ! "

Leslie, impetuously clinging to him : " Oh, thanks, thanks, thanks ! "

Bellingham, accurately focusing the pair with freshly adjusted glasses : " If you 'll both give me your blessing, now, I 'll go away, feeling perfectly rehabilitated, in the afternoon stage."

V.

Mrs. Bellingham, *and* Leslie, Blake, *and* Bellingham; *afterwards* Mrs. Murray.

Mrs. Bellingham, entering the parlor door: "Stage? Why, Mr. Blake is n't going away!"

Bellingham: "Oh, no, Mr. Blake has kindly consented to remain. It was I who thought of going. I can't bear to be idle!"

Mrs. Bellingham, apart from the others: "Charles, dear, I'm sorry I asked you to undertake that disagreeable business, and I'd have come back at once with Leslie to relieve you, — to tell you that you need n't speak after all, — but she felt sure that you would n't, and she insisted upon leaving you together and then stealing back upon you and enjoying " —

Bellingham, solemnly: "You little knew me, mother. I have the making of an iron-hearted

parent in me, and I was crushing all hope out of
Blake when Leslie came in."

Mrs. Bellingham: " Charles, you don't mean that
you said anything to wound the feelings of a man
to whom you owed your life, — to whom we *all*
owe so much ? "

Bellingham: " I don't know about his *feelings.*
But I represented pretty distinctly to him the
social incompatability."

Mrs. Bellingham: " Charles, I wonder at you ! "

Bellingham: " Oh, yes ! So do I. But if
you 'll take the pains to recall the facts, that 's exactly what you left me to do. May I ask what has
caused you to change your mind ? "

Mrs. Bellingham, earnestly : " I found that Leslie's happiness really depended upon it; and in
fact, Charles, when I came to reflect, I found that
I myself liked him."

Bellingham: " The words have a familiar sound,
— as if I had used them myself in a former existence." Turning from his mother and looking
about: " I seem to miss a — a support — moral

12

support — in those present. Where is aunt Kate?"

Mrs. Murray, appearing at the door: "Marion! Ma" — She hesitates at sight of the peaceful grouping.

Bellingham: "Ah, this is indeed opportune! Come in, aunt Kate, come in! This is a free fight, as they say in Mr. Blake's section. Any one can join." Mrs. Murray advances wonderingly into the room, and Bellingham turns to his sister, where she stands at Blake's side: "Leslie, you think I've behaved very unhandsomely in this matter, don't you?"

Leslie, plaintively: "Charley, you know I hate to blame you. But I never could have believed it if any one else had told me."

Bellingham: "All right. Mother, I understand that you would have been similarly incredulous?"

Mrs. Bellingham: "I know that you acted from ɹ good motive, Charles, but you certainly went to an extreme that I could never have expected."

Bellingham: "All right, again. Blake, if the persons and relations had all been changed, could you have said to me what I said to you?"

Blake: " That is n't a fair question, Bellingham."

Bellingham: " All right,. as before. Now, aunt Kate, I appeal to you. You know all the circumstances in which I was left here with this man who saved my life, who rescued Leslie from those tramps, who has done you all a thousand kindnesses of various sorts and sizes, who has behaved with the utmost delicacy and discretion throughout, and is in himself a thoroughly splendid fellow. Do you think I did right or wrong to set plainly before him the social disadvantages to which his marrying Leslie would put us ? "

Mrs. Murray, instantly and with great energy : " Charles, *I* say — and every person in society, *except* your mother and sister, would say — that you did exactly right ! "

Bellingham: " That settles it. Blake, my dear old fellow, I beg your pardon with all my heart; and I ask you to forget, if you can, every word I said. Confound society ! " He offers his hand to Blake, who seizes it and wrings it in his own.

Leslie, as she flings her arms round his neck,

with a fluttering cry of joy: "Oh, Charley,
Charley, I've got my ideal back again!"

Bellingham, disengaging her arms and putting
her hand into Blake's: "Both of them." Turning
to Mrs. Murray: "And now, aunt, I beg *your*
pardon. What do you say?"

Mrs. Murray, frozenly: "Charles, you know
my principles."

Bellingham: "They're identical on all points
with my own. Well?"

Mrs. Murray, grimly: "Well, then, you know
that I never would abandon my family, whatever
happened!"

Bellingham: "By Jove, that is n't so bad. We
must be satisfied to take your forgiveness as we
get it. Perhaps Leslie might object to the formula-
tion of" —

Leslie, super-joyously: "Oh, no! I object to
nothing in the world, now, Charles. Aunt Kate
is *too* good! I never should have thought of asking her to remain with us."

Bellingham: That is n't so bad, either! You
are your aunt's own niece. Come, Blake, we

can't let this go on. Say something to allay the ill feeling you 've created in this family."

Blake: "I think I 'd better not try. But if you 'll give me time, I 'll do my best to live down the objections to me."

Bellingham: "Oh, you 've done that. What we want now — as I understand aunt Kate — is that you should live down the objections to us. One thing that puzzles me " — thoughtfully scratching the sparse parting of his hair — " is that our position is so very equivocal in regard to the real principle involved. It seems to me that we are begging the whole question, which is, if Blake " —

Leslie: "There, there! I *knew* he would! "

Bellingham, severely: "Mother, you will allow that I have been left to take the brunt of this little affair in a — well, somewhat circuitous manner? "

Mrs. Bellingham: "Charles, I am very, very sorry " —

Bellingham: "And that I am entitled to some sort of reparation? "

Leslie : " Don't allow that, mamma! I know he's going to say something disagreeable. He looks just as he always does when he has one of his ideas."

Bellingham : " Thanks, Miss Bellingham. I am going to have this particular satisfaction out of *you.* Then I will return to my habitual state of agreeable vacancy. Mother " —

Leslie : " Mamma, don't answer him! It's the only way."

Bellingham : " It is not necessary that I should be answered. I only wish to have the floor. The question is, if Blake were merely a gentleman somewhat at odds with his history, associations, and occupation, and not also our benefactor and preserver in so many ways, — whether we should be so ready to — ah " —

Mrs. Bellingham : " Charles, dear, I think it is unnecessary to enter into these painful minutiæ."

Mrs. Murray : " I feel bound to say that I know we should not."

Bellingham : " This is the point which I wished to bring out. Blake, here is your opportunity : renounce us !"

Blake : " What do you say, Leslie ? "

Leslie : "I say that I don't believe it, and I know that I like you for yourself, — not for what you've done for us. I did from the first moment, before you spoke or saw me. But if you doubt me, or should ever doubt me " —

Blake, taking in his left both the little hands that she has appealingly laid upon his arms : " That 's out of the question ! "

www.ingramcontent.com/pod-product-compliance
Lightning Source LLC
Chambersburg PA
CBHW022356020726
47500CB00002B/308